Henry James Byron

Sensation Dramas for the Back Drawing Room

Vol. 1

Henry James Byron

Sensation Dramas for the Back Drawing Room
Vol. 1

ISBN/EAN: 9783337375898

Printed in Europe, USA, Canada, Australia, Japan

Cover: Foto ©Andreas Hilbeck / pixelio.de

More available books at **www.hansebooks.com**

SENSATION DRAMAS

BACK DRAWING ROOM.

BY

HENRY J. BYRON,

AUTHOR OF

The Old Story; Dundreary Married and Done For; Cinderella; Blue Beard from a New Point of Hue; Robinson Crusoe; Mazeppa; The Maid and the Magpie, or the Fatal Spoon; The Babes in the Wood; Bride of Abydos; Fra Diavolo; Jack the Giant Killer; Very Latest Edition of the Lady of Lyons; The Nymph of the Lurleyberg; Pilgrim of Love; The Garibaldi Excursionists; Aladdin, or the Wonderful Scamp; Esmeralda, or the Sensation Goat; Goldenhair the Good; Ivanhoe in Accordance, etc.; Beauty and the Beast; Rival Othellos; Whittington and his Cat; Puss in a New Pair of Boots; Miss Lily O'Connor; George de Barnwell; Our Sea-side Lodgings; The Rosebud of Stinging-nettle Farm; The Sensation Fork; My Wife and I; Beautiful Haidee, or the Sea Nymph and the Sallee Rovers; Ill Treated Il Trovatore; The Motto: "I am all there!" St. George and the Dragon; Lady Belle Belle; Orpheus and Eurydice, or the Young Gentleman who charmed the Rocks; 1863, or the Sensations of the Past Year; Mazourka, or the Stick, the Pole, and the Tartar; The "Grin" Bushes; &c., &c.

PART AUTHOR OF

The Miller and his Men; Valentine and Orson; & Forty Thieves (Savage Club).

LONDON:
SAMUEL FRENCH,
PUBLISHER,
89. STRAND.

NEW YORK:
SAMUEL FRENCH & SON,
PUBLISHERS.
122. NASSAU STREET.

C

EXPLANATION OF THE STAGE DIRECTIONS.

The Actor is supposed to face the Audience.

	D. R. C.	C. D.	D. L. C.	

R. U. E.		Scene.		L. U. E.
R. 3 E.				L. 3 E.
R. 2 E.				L. 2 E.
R. 1 E.				L. 1 E.
R.	R. C.	C.	L. C.	L.

Audience.

L.	Left.	**C.**	Centre.
L. C.	Left Centre.	**R.**	Right.
L. 1 E.	Left First Entrance.	**R. 1 E.**	Right First Entrance.
L. 2 E.	Left Second Entrance.	**R. 2 E.**	Right Second Entrance.
L. 3 E.	Left Third Entrance.	**R. 3 E.**	Right Third Entrance.
L. U. E.	Left Upper Entrance (wherever the Scene may be.)	**R. U. E.**	Right Upper Entrance.
D. L. C.	Door Left Centre.	**D. R. C.**	Door Right Centre.

SENSATION DRAMAS

FOR THE

BACK DRAWING ROOM .

MATEUR THEATRI-
CALS are the rage of the
age. Back drawing rooms
pass an abnormal existence,
and are as frequently the
receptacle of Lilliputian
scenery and infinitesimal
properties, as they are of
the articles of *vertu, bijou-
terie,* and elegant parapher-
nalia proper to their original
condition. "Lines of business" are now apportioned
to the young men on the
visiting list, from the "respectable utility" of the Govern-
ment neophyte to the "heavy business" of the bouncing
dragoon. All this is very good fun, and to further the
movement, we publish a series of Sensation Dramas
suitable for rough-and-ready amateurs, who are willing
to make noodles of themselves for the amusement of their
friends, or in the far more commendable cause of charity.

CONTENTS.

THE
RIVAL RAJAHS OF RAMJAM COODLUM;
OR,
SIKHS OF ONE AND HALF-A-DOZEN OF THE OTHER.

A GRAND ORIENTAL SPECTACLE OF INDIFFERENCE.

Characters.

MEAMBLACKANDTAN SINGH.
PICCALILLA *(his Daughter)*.
RUMTIFOOZLE SINGH.
CHOW CHOW *(his Son)*.

SCENE FIRST.—*The Plains of India. The Bogs of Barrampoota seen stretching away into the far distance. Cotton-fields of Chutney on the left, and the Indian Pickle Groves on the right.*

N.B.—This Scene will be flavoured with Rimmel's Toilet Vinegar.

Chorus of common FELLAHS, *who are engaged in picking the remunerative and fragrant native quarrel as the curtain rises.*

   Hark! 'tain't the Indian drum!
     Tum te tum.
   And nobody don't come:
     Tum te tum.
   No, 'tain't the Indian drum,
   By Jingo, and by gum!
    The woods and rocks around,
    Do not at all resound.
   No, 'tain't the Indian drum:
   Tum, tum, te tum, te tum, te tum.

  (CHORUS *repeat the burden, which they also carry off, leaving the stage to darkness, and to* MEAMBLACKANDTAN SINGH, *who enters moodily,* L. U. E.; *he looks for a round, which the obtuse audience, not recognizing him, do not award him*)

MEAMB. Twice twenty Indian summers have rolled by
  Since from my couch I, a mere stripling, stept—

For I had nothing on.
A bare subsistence then indeed was mine ;
A cold unfeeling world was all around ;
A draught came underneath the nursery door ;
And chilled and blighted in my infant hopes,
Ticket-of-leave like, quite dishearten'd, I
Sneered at the honest—and returned to crib.
Here in my palace, pampered and fed up,
Until in plumpness I resemble more
The pattern animal in Baker Street,
Which annually with its magic pen,
Draws the metropolis and farming fry—
Than the rich King of Ramjam Coodlum, here
I drag out an existence mis'rable,
With one fair daughter, sole and only prop
Of my declining years, my Piccalilla.
If I could see her comfortably settled,
It would, indeed—as I observed last year,
When they my health proposed with nine times nine—
Be—yes—the proudest moment of my life.
But on the borders of my territory—
Which, by the way, is marked, and here's the mark—
(indicating a chalk line drawn down the stage)
There dwells the Rajah Rumtifoozle Singh ;
A lean and hungry Rajah, with an eye
Upon my broad possessions, while on his
I throw a glance of envy and desire.
I would have *his* as well as mine, and *he*
Would add *my* land to *his* ter-rit-to-REE.
(walks up and down his territory)

Enter on the opposite side of the stage, R., the RAJAH RUMTIFOOZLE SINGH, *a tall spare party, in every way opposed to the* RAJAH MEAMBLACKANDTAN SINGH.

RUMTI. (*not perceiving the other*) Now is the winter of
   For foul is fair, to be or not to be, [our discontent,
With interest at sixty-five per cent.
   May and December never can agree.
Pity the sorrows of a poor old man,
   " Whose sands of life" are nearly all expended,
To quote the advertised physici-an ;

'Twill cost you two-and-six to get it mended.
Last night a most terrific thunderstorm
  Broke over the Metropolis; mule twist
Is active, administrative reform.
  The ballot, Chiltern Hundreds, and the list
Of voters for the county. Hearts are trumps.
  The charge against him was completely proved,
And when the Surrey players drew their stumps,
  The wretched prisoner was then removed.
    Pray, silence in the court, that dreadful bell; ⎫
    The worst of walnuts, they're so hard to shell; ⎬
    And Freedom shrieked when Kosciusco fell. ⎭
    (*overcome by his emotions, the* RAJAH *blows his nose*)
MEAMB. Another blow, and I return it, mind.
RUMTI. What! Rajah Ramjam! Are you really there?
MEAMB. I are; and Ramjam in your teeth, false caitiff!
RUMTI. (*scornfully*) I can afford to laugh at thee.
MEAMB. (*quickly*)   Oh, yes;
  But that is all you can afford to do.
RUMTI. My poverty, and not my will, consents
  To pocket, Ramjam, that there insolence.
MEAMB. (*more quickly*) 'Tis all that you *can* pocket, you're
  Your treasury is empty, and your crown.   [aware;
  You know's in pawn, and not upawn your head.
RUMTI. Oh, if I dare invade your kingdom, I
  Would—but no matter.
MEAMB.   That's the case with me.
  Could I but enter without trespassing.
  I'd walk into your empire and to you.
RUMTI. I will invade it! To yourself, pray, look—
  This insolence I will not G. V. Brooke.
                (*rushes off like Othello,* R.)
  MEAMB. (*shouts after him at the top of his stentorian
voice*) I pity and despise you! And now to fortify the
citadel. (*goes off,* L.)

    Enter PICCALILLA, *his daughter.* L. U. E.

PICCA. Where is my Chow Chow, monarch of my heart,
  And likewise heir-apparent to the throne
  Of our dire enemy and bitter foe,
  The Rajah Rumtifoozle? Chow Chow!

Enter PRINCE CHOW CHOW *in the dominions of* RUMTI-
                   FOOZLE, R.

CHOW.   Here !
    "It is the East, and Juliet is the sun."

PICCA. My love, were I at all inclined to pun,
    Which I am not, as you're away, I'd say,
    It isn't July yet; it's only May.

CHOW. The month, my darling, when "a young man's
        fancy,"
    (E'en the street urchins "wish they were with Nancy,")
    "Turns lightly," Tennyson observes, "to love."
    By Jove—or say, to meet the rhyme—"by Juv!"
    I swear I love thee, and thou must be mine.

PICCA. The course of true love aye was serpentine.
    Remember that our parents——

CHOW.   Name them not,
    Or see your Chow Chow perish on the spot!
    Fathers have flinty hearts; let us away,
    The curfew tolls the knell of parting day.

(N.B.—*This is not the case, but the author could not resist the rhyme,*
    which the reader is requested to excuse.

    (*the* LOVERS *embrace, and, coming down to the foot-*
    lights, sing the following)

                 Duet.

TOGETHER. Two wretched lovers, we'll run away
        Far from the plains of this hot Indi—ay;

England's the home of the fond and the free—
Chow.   England for me—
Picca.   And for me—
Both.   Yes, for we.
                         England !
(*echo on the flute*)   Merry England !
(*more echo*) Yes, England's the Queen of the Sea !

Recitative.

When the wolf with nightly prowl,
And the solemn midnight owl,
Merrily dance the quaker's wife,
Oh, a life on the ocean wave, a life
On the ocean wave !
Yes, a pirate's grave,
A home on the rolling deep ;
For men must work and women must weep,
When they've got a family to keep,
To keep, to keep, to (*very low*) keep.

Picca. (*continuing the recitative*)
        Shades of evening, close not o'er us ;
(*aside, to* Chow Chow)
        Let us hope they won't encore us.
        Take this cup of sparkling wine ;
        Coals to Newcastle-on-Tyne
        Are quiet superfluous, you know ;
        Mrs. Harriet Beecher Stowe.
        Yes, we fly by night,
        Though it isn't right ;
        We'll away to the mountain's brow,
        Where I'll register a vow
        To be Mrs., yes, Mrs. Chow (*very high*) Chow !

Together. Then away, away,
        Ere the break of day ;
          Away to the forest heather,
        Where we'll dance and sing,
        And dull care we'll fling
          Away while we sing together.
              Tra la la la,
              Tra la la la,
              Tra la la lal lido,

Tra la la lá,
Tra la la la,
Tra la la lal lido!

[This Chorus is registered.]

Exeunt PRINCE, R., PICCALILLA, L., *opposite sides.*

Grand march—Enter on RUMTIFOOZLE'S *territory,* L., *a
grand Procession—first an Elephant bearing the* BAND,
who play out of a pavilion and tune, then a body of SUPERS
with very blue chins, and with their eyes fixed on the STAGE
MANAGER, *who is at the wing directing them—they are
painfully depressed with the consciousness of not looking
a bit like what they are intended to represent, but bear
up manfully nevertheless—the Procession on* MEAM-
BLACKANDTAN'S *side of the stage then enters,* L.—*he also
leads off with an Elephant, with a* BAND, *if possible, more
out of tune than the other*)

Flourish, and enter the two RAJAHS, R. *and* L.

RUMTI. (*to his men*) Thus far into the bowels of the land
(The allegory you will understand)
Have I marched on, and now I halt to view
My adversary.
MEAMB. (*to his men*) Halt! Harrup-haroo!
(*this is military for* "Right front forward," *or*
"Rear rank, take open disorder," *or something
else of the same kind*)

MEAMB. *(to his men)* My brave companions, partners of
    My feelings, and my fame. I'm loth to spoil [my toil,
    Those uniforms, for which I have to pay
    A very heavy sum to Mr. May ;
    But when the blast of war blows in our ears,
    'Twere cowardly to talk of costumiers.
    So on to victory like heroes fight ;
    Your Rajah will retire and watch the sight.
    Form ! (*the* ARMY *rattle their weapons and prepare*)
RUMTI. Are you ready ? Treat your foes with scorn—
MEAMB. Hah ! by the pricking of my Indian corn,
    There's something this way comes. Quick ! Draw !

PICCALILLA *rushes in,* L. U. E., *and throws herself before her
    father.*

MEAMB.   My child !
PICCA. Dear father, I entreat you, draw it mild.
RUMTI. (*to his troops*) Prepare to charge !

CHOW CHOW *rushes on,* L. U. E., *and throws himself before his
    father.*

    To charge ! Halloa, young man.
CHOW. Dear father, charge as little as you can.
MEAMB. What means this conduct, girl ?
RUMTI.   Young man, how now !
MEAMB. Speak, Piccalilla, love.
RUMTI.   Speak, dear Chow Chow.
PICCA. Pardon me, father ; but we're married.

MEAMB. Eh?

CHOW. Legitimately, in the reg'lar way.

You wouldn't kill your daughter-in law's 'pa?

PICCA. You wouldn't kill your son-in-law's——

THE RIVAL RAJAHS. (*simultaneously*) Ha! ha!

(*they look at each other, then at their children, and
then rush into each other's arms*)

(*the* BRIDE *and* BRIDEGROOM *kneel*)

MTI. Bless you——

MEAMB. My children. And if you (*to Audience*) will smile
Upon our humble efforts to beguile
Ten minutes' tedium, there will nothing **be**
Wanting to com-plete the felicity
Of Meamblackandtan.

RUMTI. And—let me - add—
There won't in India dwell a happier dad
Than Rumtifoozle.

CHOW. Oh, what bliss in view!

PICCA. May every Indian lover be as true.
Our once fierce parents at each other grin;
One touch of nature makes the whole world kin.

(*the* SIKHS *of one, overcome by emotion, break
through the boundary line, and insist upon em-
bracing the half-a-dozen of the other, and upon
a scene of mutual forgiveness — and entente
Godfrey Cordiale-ism—the Curtain descends*)

THE McALLISTER McVITTY McNAB;

OR, THE

LAIRD, THE DAFTIE, AND THE HIGHLAND MAIDEN.

(A CALEDONIAN DRAMA.)

Characters.

| THE LAIRD. | THE DAFTIE. | SOLDIERS. |
| A VISITOR. | FLORA. | RETAINERS. |

SCENE.—*The Banks and Braes of Glengarry, in the heart of Mid Cockpen, on the mountainous estate of the outlawed Laird of Bonny Doon. The Marmalade plant of Dundee grows in wild profusion, and the Toddy-tree shades the right hand of the stage. The ruined walls of the Laird's home are covered with the national creeper.*

The LAIRD *and his* VISITOR *are seated at a more than ordinarily rude table, carousing.*

LAIRD. And so you like our simple customs?

VISITOR. (*helping himself to his fifth glass of toddy*) I do. The artificial heat of the crowded *salon*, the warm debates of the Senate, the fiery eloquence of the Bar, have no charms for me. Give me the bracing breezes of the Highlands, the genuine hospitality of the North Briton, the unsophisticated whiskey of the uncultivated wilds. (*drinks*)

LAIRD. Ha, boy, it not only warms my cockles, but invigorates my muscles, to hear you expatiate with so much eloquence on my humble efforts to make your stay here pleasurable. I am—you are aware—an outlaw.

VISITOR. As you have communicated that fact to me, on an average, six times an hour during my three days' visit, I think I may with safety say that I *am* aware of it.

LAIRD. The Sassenachs—but no matter.

VISITOR. (*hastily*) Certainly not; don't mention it.

LAIRD. Why should I inflict upon you the tale of my wrongs?

VISITOR. Ah, why indeed?

LAIRD. And yet—I will.

VISITOR. No, no, not on any account; its recapitulation will distress you.

LAIRD. (*tearfully*) No, no, it does me good. One night——

VISITOR. (*aside, piteously*) **Oh dear!**

LAIRD. I was sleeping——

VISITOR. In your orchard?

LAIRD. No; in the back kitchen. I had been smoking, and my wife objected to tobacco in the drawing room. I awoke—to find myself proscribed—proclaimed a traitor, my goods confiscated, a price set on my head, and oh!—but let me not think of it. Here, Daftie, sing something, for these bitter memories make me mad. (*DAFTIE comes forward—he is a ragged Scotch dependant, suggesting by his outer man a hungry Isle of Skye terrier, who has not been treated as a pet; and his looks combine the idiotcy of the proverbial Silly Billy, and the cunning of the more self-evidently villanous Iagos*)

DAFTIE. Heh, hech, spracchan, pibroch, McSassenach, bodach, hurrrrrooh?

LAIRD. The faithful creature asks us, in his somewhat dislocated Gaelic, "What shall he have the pleasure of obliging the company with?"

VISITOR. Oh! anything that's lively. (*the HEAD PIPER comes forward to accompany DAFTIE—several of the RETAINERS gather round*)

The Wail of the Daftie.

Oh. hone arie !
German hone arie !
McSpleuchen is nae mair,
And eh my hairt is sair.
Let his shroud be warrior's plaidie,
Fit for sic a winsome laddie ;
Athol Brose and Finnin Haddie,
Oh, hone arie !

(*all the* RETAINERS *join in a repetition of the concluding lines*)

2nd verse.

Oh, hone arie !
All alone arie !
Mc Spleuchen's gane, ye ken,
He'll nae come bock agen ;
Never looked up sin his marriage,
And his wife would hae her carriage,
Kinahan and oatmeal parridge.
Oh, hone arie !

(*the* LAIRD *waves his hand to the* SINGER *as a sign that he will dispense with the remaining forty-seven verses—the* SINGERS *retire*)

LAIRD. Help yourself, and don't mind me. As for myself, I will e'en lay my weary limbs upon a warrior's best bed—the floor. (*the* LAIRD *lays his claymore down as a pillow, and drawing his kilt tightly round him, sleeps*)

VISITOR. (*looking round*) The arch-traitor sleeps. He little dreams that—but soft, my men must be short of air. (*goes to trap or secret door, which he opens*)

Several SOLDIERS *appear almost exhausted ; they have been taking turns to place their mouths at the crack in the stage, and have thus barely succeeded in supporting life—on the trap being raised, they all give a prolonged gasp.*

VISITOR. The arch-traitor is in a heavy slumber. Have you your ammunition ready ?

SERGEANT. Yes, captain.

VISITOR. How many are there of you?

SERGEANT. Twenty.

VISITOR. Are you all loaded up to the muzzle?

SERGEANT. (*apoplectically from long confinement*) We are—busting.

VISITOR. And our foe is but one poor, weak, elderly Scotchman. (*taps his breast heroically*) It shall be done. Come up! (*all the* SOLDIERS *rise from trap*) Now then, make ready. (SOLDIERS *make ready*) Present! (SOLDIERS *present*) F—— (*before the* VISITOR *can utter the word,* FLORA MC DONALD MC ALLISTER MCVITTY MC NAB *enters,* L., *and draws the claymore suddenly from beneath her father's head—the parental "nob" comes on to the boards with a sharp crack, but its owner still sleeps*)

FLORA. One step further and this trusty claymore rids the world of (*rapidly counting them*) twenty-one ungrateful r-r-r-r-r-r-r-r-r-r-r-wretches!

VISITOR. (*to his men*) And so ye hang back before a timid gee-yurl! Pretty soldiers *you* are! Fire! (*the* SOLDIERS *murmur*) Now, then, are you going to obey your superior officer?

SERGEANT. (*weatherbeaten*) Beg pardon, captain, but she —she's—a gal.

VISITOR. (*losing his temper in the confusion of the moment*) Oh indeed: a gal, is she? A court-martial for *you*, my man, as sure as my name's Wilkins. (FLORA MC DONALD MC ALLISTER MCVITTY MCNAB *turns pale, drops the claymore, and sinks on to a three-legged stool*) Now, then; now that she's dropped the weapon and can't resist, I suppose you'll refuse to obey orders? Fire immediately. (SOLDIERS *murmur more than ever*) I tell you what it is; you'll have the father waking up in a minute; you'd better obey orders.

CORPORAL. (*browned by service*) Your honour, if we was a seeing you a walking into the jaws of destruction, we'd follow you until you was in 'em with faithfulness and pleasure; but as to shooting at a woman—a British soldier! Never. You may tear my head from my shoulders and punch my stripes, but I won't do it—there!

THE REMAINING NINETEEN MEN. Hurray!

VISITOR. (*aside*) This honest fellow has unmanned me for the moment, but I am once more myself.　　Present!

MISS MC NAB. Wilkins!

VISITOR. (*changing his tone*) Hah!

MISS MC NAB. Wilkins! It comes across mine ear like an almost forgotten strain of the ancle ; Wilkins!

VISITOR. Pshaw! it is impossible. Seize her! (*is about to seize her when the* DAFTIE *enters with a huge cudgel and levels him with the earth—the stage is simultaneously covered with* HIGHLANDERS)

DAFTIE. " Upon what meat doth this our seizer feed,
　　　　That he is grown so great ?"

Hem! Shakspeare.

VISITOR. Horror! that voice!

MISS MC NAB. Agony! Them accents! (*suddenly remembering her position, and the large sums which have been expended on her education*) *Those* accents!

ALL THE FEMALE SUPERNUMERARIES (*dropping their very doubtful Gaelic, in the surprise of the moment*) Lawks!

MALE SUPERS. A Daisy!

MALES AND FEMALES. Dickens!

THE DAFTIE. (*retiring, and almost immediately re-appearing in the modern female costume*) Yes, together with my assumed garments, do I discard my false appellation. I am not a daftie ; I am as sane as anybody. Look upon this worn and haggard countenance, Wilkins. Do you not remember the features of your deserted wife? (*consternation*)

B

Visitor. Anna Maria! My first, my only love! Tell me—in pity, tell me, have you—have you left off that disagreeable habit of insisting upon the last word?

Mrs. Wilkins. Days of loneliness and nights of lumbago have worn my suffering spirits to the bone. I have.

Wilkins. (*for further concealment is unnecessary*) Anna Maria! come to a soldier's arms! (*indicating his sword and musket*) Stay—one word—that young girl—

Mrs. Wilkins. Is our child! It was to watch over her that I assumed the rude garb of an idiot.

Wilkins. Daughter!

Miss Wilkins. Father! (*wild embrace*)

The Mc Allister Mc Vitty Mc Nab. (*rising and seeing, with the **perspicacity** of his countrymen, the whole circumstances at a glance*) And while the beautiful lesson learnt to-night must sink deeply into all your three hearts, let us hope our kind friends in front may fully appreciate the great truths that "a man's a man for a' that," that "gin a body meet a body need—I say *need*—a body cry?"

> (*all the Characters dance a Cock-a-Leekie to a spirited performance by a native piper on the Tulloch gore 'em (or cattle horn)—the* Laird *does the celebrated Heeland toe figure in the front as the curtain comes down, with evident reluctance*)

"TAFFY WAS A WELSHMAN;"

OR,

THE CHILD, THE CHOUSE, AND THE CHEESE.

A Cambrian Drama.

Characters.

AP THOMAS AP SHENKIN AP MORGAN AP JONES (*a Welshman*).
TAFFY (*a Thief*).
JENNY (*the "Cream of the Valley"*).

WELSH IRRITATION.

SCENE.—*The home of Ap Thomas at the foot of Plinsnowdonmawr, in the Valley of Llanmachynllthllw. Through the open window PEASANTS are seen picking Llanberris from an ancestral tree in the back garden. The prints of Wales are suspended from various hooks on the walls.*

AP THOMAS AP SHENKIN AP MORGAN AP JONES *seated at a table prepared for supper; AP THOMAS is also prepared for supper, and is whirling his knife about to impress the audience that he is a flourishing farmer.*

B 2

AP THOMAS. Now then! is that supper coming? Is the largest farmer for miles round, the proprietor of more than three acres of mountainous territory—one who keeps two pigs, a cow, three farming lads, and a girl to churn, not to have his supper at the time he orders it? (*gradually works himself into a state of maniacal fury; the veins of his forehead dilate upon his remarks, his eyes flash in a manner that throws the candles into the shade, from which they are picked out and replaced in their sockets by a careful attendant—he bares his gums up to the elbow, and appears on the very point of getting irritated, when the "Cream of the Valley," JENNY, enters, L., with a dish of toasted cheese, and the combined effects of woman's presents and nature's gifts are immediately evident in his comparative coolness—viewing the dish*) Hah! this *is* the cheese!

JENNY. Father, I have gathered it with my own fair fingers.

AP THOMAS. There is not much of it, my child; but such as there is is strong.

JENNY. Yes, dear father; our bracing mountain air is not without its effect upon the toothsome edible in question. But, dear father, you have often said you would clear up the mystery which surrounds me; there cannot be a fitter opportunity than the present. Who am I?

AP THOMAS. Loved one, I am exceedingly hungry, and the favourite food of my native clime has a disagreeable knack of getting somewhat suddenly cool; therefore the present is *not* a happy moment to select for telling you the mysterious story of your infancy.

JENNY. Father, I have stood this awful suspense for eighteen years, two months, a week, and three days—it is wearing me to the bone!

> (*at the word* "bone," AP THOMAS *chokes, and loses his breath and articulation in a mingled flood of Welsh ale and consonants*)

AP THOMAS. (*recovering himself*) Bone! say marrow-bone at once! Ha! ha! ha! Say marrow-bone at once!
> (*sinks into a chair and despondency*)

JENNY. (*surprised, but innocently*) "Say marrow-bone

at once!" Certainly, dear father, if you wish it:—marrow-bone.

AP THOMAS. (*rising enraged*) Girl! Fiendess in Winsey Lonsey—leastways, Cardinal Linsey—no, Wolsey —no, Wonsey Linsey—no! Oh, these bitter memories! (*buries himself in the past*)

[To Provincial Managers and Others (especially "others.") *The mechanical process by which Ap Thomas buries himself in the past is registered A 1 at Lloyd's, is entered at Stationers' Hall, and may be procured at most respectable chemists. N.B.—See that there is no label on the bottle, or you will probably obtain a spurious article*]

JENNY. How sad a sight it is to see a parent bowed down by the oblivious recollection of a bygone future, with his tears dropping sadly in the mustard, and the caseous compound an affectionate daughter has prepared congealing like the Lake of Bala beneath the biting frosts of Father Winter. I will see if one of the wild ditties of the barbaric past will have the effect of smoothing the wrinkles on his distempered brow. (*takes a harp down from the wall and commences*)

> Dim Sassenach,
> Dim Sassenach,
> Ruin seize thee, ruthless king!
> Toasted cheese is no bad thing.
> Caroo Dha.
> Ha! ha! ha!
> Barra cous,
> Welshers chouse,
> Confusion on thy banners wait.
> Bring, oh, bring another plate!
> In our mountains, in our vales,
> In our ponies, in our ales,
> In our wigs and milking pails,
> See, oh see, the Pride of Wales,
> The Pride, the Pri—i—i—i—ide of Wales.

(*the effect of the song upon the parent is not of the soothing nature expected, and on its conclusion he seizes his daughter's wrist wildly*)

AP THOMAS. (*excitedly*) My child, he was my countryman, my friend!

But, I regret to add, his practices
Were of a nature not supposed to be
As honest as they might have been ; in fact,
To speak the truth, my child, he *was a thief!*
He came to *my* house—mark me, girl, to *mine*—
And from the larder basely did purloin
A portion of—*he stole a piece of beef.*
Stung with the act and panting for revenge,
I went to *his* house—mark me, girl, to *his ;*
But with a coward's instincts full in force,
Taffy'd retired—yes, *he was not at home !*
When I returned, oh, agony and shame !
Can I forget the deed of that dark night ?
He had to *my* house come when I was out,
And actually *stole a marrow bone !*
Years have rolled on since that eventful day,
But now the time for vengeance has arrived !
Taffy's one child was stolen in the night !
Ha ! ha ! He ! he !—no matter. Here he comes.

Enter TAFFY, L.

TAFFY. Ap Thomas, what is the meaning of this
mysterious invitation ?

AP THOMAS. Taffy, years have rolled by since twenty
years ago.

TAFFY. They have—twenty of them.

JENNY. (*aside*) What strange sensation is this which
overcomes me ? (*pause—a note higher*) I say, what
strange sensation is this which overcomes me ? (*there is
no reply, and* JENNY, *disgusted, retires up stage and sulks*)

AP THOMAS. (*to* TAFFY) Look on yon young girl.
What do you think of her ?

TAFFY. Nothing.

AP THOMAS. Humph ! You had a child ?

TAFFY. I had ; of the female sex.

AP THOMAS. A girl, in short.

TAFFY. "The werry identical flute."

AP THOMAS. (*aside*) A quotation, I believe, from one
of our early bards ; but I will not notice it. (*to* TAFFY)
A doubly-dyed ruffian stole that child.

TAFFY. Oh, dear no, not at all ; a very considerate

person walked off with the infant, and most kindly undertook to bring her up, taking the entire trouble and responsibility upon his own shoulders. Bless him!

AP THOMAS. What—what, I say, if that person were to restore your child to you?

TAFFY. Well, I wouldn't own her.

AP THOMAS. Oh, Nature, Nature! how wonderful are thy ramifications! Should you know her again?

TAFFY. Oh, yes; she'd a strong cast in her left ear, squinted with both feet, lisped when walking, and would insist upon wearing her eyelashes in ringlets. She was in the constant habit of plucking the fairest flower, and she never told her love.

AP THOMAS. (aside) The same, the same, indeed. Jenny!

TAFFY. (aside) That name! That uncommon name! Can it be she? It is.

AP THOMAS. (to JENNY) Have you any recollection of your parent?

JENNY. Oh, dear father, you have always been a parent to me. I would know no other.

AP THOMAS. Not if you were to see him?

JENNY. Don't—the very idea chills me to the—(is about to say bone, but recollecting the recent parental outbreak, substitutes)—very blood!

[Will some one inform us, by the way, what is the peculiar distinctive quality of " very" blood. Is it of a more decided colour than " rather" blood? But this by the way.]

AP THOMAS. What was he like? Describe his outer man.

JENNY. A low forehead with beetle brows, high cheek bones, deeply-sunken eyes (not pairs), hoarse voice, bull-neck, and the entire countenance a combination of the strongest-marked ruffianism, and the weakest possible imbecility.

TAFFY. (with an irrepressible burst of fatherly feeling) The darling has not forgotten me!

JENNY. Hah! (after a pause) Pa!

AP THOMAS. You see your child—take her.

TAFFY. Nay; you would not crush a fallen man?

Ap Tho ᵐas. I have registered a vow to have revenge, and you must take her.

Taffy. Have pity on my grey hairs!

Ap Thᵘmas. What pity had you on my Sunday's dinner, my peace of mind, my piece of beef?

Taffy Oh, 'orrid recollection!

Jenny (*through her tears*) Horrid!

Taffy My own child correcting me! Hagony!

Jenny (*broken by emotion*) Hem! Agony!

Taffy This, indeed, is retribution. (*weeps*)

Ap Thomas. They weep. The sight unmans me. I will achieve a brilliant conquest over my own bad feelings. I WILL NEVER PART WITH HER. (Jenny *and* Taffy *come up smiling*) Come to these arms. (Jenny *comes to them*)

Taffy. (*an altered man*) AND THIS IS ELEANOR'S VICTORY.

> (*the orchestra strikes up a selection of national hares and Welsh rabbits.* ATTENDANTS *enter with the* **bread,** *and the curtain descends with a roll*)

GREEN GROW THE RUSHES, OH;

OR,

THE SQUIREEN, THE INFORMER, AND THE ILLICIT DISTILLER.

A HIBERNIAN SENSATION DRAMA.

Dedicated to Messrs. Boucicault, Falconer, and other gentlemen, who have recently given us such an insight into the local habits and customs of the "bold peasantry, a country's pride"—together with the ordinary conduct of the Clergy and the Upper Classes.

Characters.

MILES NA BOCLISH.
THE SQUIREEN DON'T CAREY.
THE RIVD. PHADRIG O'SHOCKNESSY.
MICHAEL MULLIGAN.
CAPTAIN CLUTTERBUCK.
EILY O'PHILLILOO.
PEASANTRY (*bold and retiring*).

ACT I.

SCENE.—*The Wakes of Bogtrotterly. Lively music as curtain rises on a scene of revelry—*R. *of stage,* BLIND PADDY *playing his fiddle from music which is held for him by* MCSWEENY, *a discharged sailor who has lost both arms at the battle of the Boyne—*WHISKEY PAT *has his tent pitched (not painted) on* L. *side, and is boldly vending unlicensed whiskey, fifty degrees above proof, to "ould* NICK DALEY," *the gauger—the* PEASANTS *are all ragged, with large open night gown collars, and have shillelaghs; the* PEASANTESSES *have black hair, in tight braids close to the head, red cloaks, and grey stockings over the trimmest possible ankles.*

ALL. Hurroo! (*strike their sticks on the stage and then attitudes*)

MULLIGAN. (*a hangdog-looking fellow, with haybands for garters, a red neckerchief—indispensable—and a scowl which has apparently become chronic*) Who'll tread on the tail of my coat? (*all the* PEASANTS *rush eagerly to accommodate him*)

WHISKEY PAT. Go along wid ye; ye're a good-for-nothing vagabone at the best of times. What are you doing, spoiling the lasses' pleasure at the wakes by putting in *your* ugly nose, eh? (*jumps up and flourishes his shillelagh, which, even in the busiest moments of serving the liquor, he has never relinquished*)

PEASANTS. Hurroo! give it him, Pat!

W. PAT. (*emboldened by the general support*) Who killed his grandmother for the sake of her ould silver thimble?

PEASANTS *and* PEASANTESSES, *especially* PEASANTESSES. Yaar! (*groans*)

W. PAT. Who played spy and tould the military where the fourteen kegs of whiskey was stowed away in the barn, and never spent a penny of the reward over the liquor he'd denounced.

CHORUS. (*as before, but if possible more defiantly*) Ya-a-r!

PEASANTS. Down with the informer—down with the black-hearted Mulligan!

> (*they are about to fall upon the unpopular* PEASANT *in question when the* REVD. PATRICK O'SHOCKNESSY *enters suddenly,* R.—*also with a shillelagh—and the* PARISHIONERS *drop their weapons and take off their hats*)

O'SHOCK. What, you murthering spalpeens, would ye add assassination to your other crimes? Stand off! or by the time the piper played before he changed his mind and did another, I'll knock every manjack of ye into as flat a cocked hat as ever disgraced the narrow brow of the sodgering Sassenach! Lave the dirty black-gyard alone, and let him go home to his ould mother and help her to mend her worsted stockings, and maybe he'll be able to get her to give his own hose a trifling taste of a stitch, for bedad, he's tumbling to pieces like Mother Hooligan's shebeen.

> (*roars of laughter from all the* PEASANTRY, *of course with the exception of* MULLIGAN, *who pulls his hat over his brows, walks up the avenue formed by two rows of scowling* PEASANTRY, *and exits,* R. U. E.,

*with an expression of countenance denoting a deter-
mination to be revenged on the whole human race)*

Enter EILY O'PHILLILOO. L., *followed by* MILES NA BOCLISH.
MILES *carries a small keg on his shoulder—it is not known
precisely why, but it gives "character" to the part, and
is indispensable. Provincial managers will bear this in
mind, as it is important.*

EILY. Go 'long wid your nonsense, Miles; you know I
can't marry ye.

MILES. (*with tearfulness, tinged with native humour*)
Bedad, darlint, don't I know that same? Sure isn't it the
love I wished to lavish upon ye—the milk of human kind-
ness as a body might say—that's a souring in my system
and turning my youth and innocence into curds and whey?
Oh, darlint, don't I know you can niver be mine, and isn't
it that one bright thought that makes me able to support
life. Oh, Eily, acushla, when I saw you pegging away
at the praties last evening at Mother Finnigan's, and I
remembered I hadn't a farthing in the wurrld and nothing
to support nature but an ould pair of brogues and a tinder
box, I dropped a tear as briny as the bogs of Connemara, and
blest my Stars and Dials that you was engaged to another.

EILY. (*aside*) True heart, true heart; he loves me
dearly indeed.

MILES. (*looking into her eyes*) When I gaze into the
deep blue of thim eyes, mavourneen, I haven't the remotest
compunction in telling you that I wouldn't have you if
there wasn't another woman in the world. (*retires*)

EILY. Ah! would the heartless lovers in polite society
possessed the honest truthfulness of the simple Irish
peasant.

(*Dance—*EILY, *at first listless, but on the appear-
ance of young* SQUIREEN DON'T CAREY, R., *she
wakes up, and enters into the joviality of the scene—*
MILES *cuts in, and, becoming excited, takes off
his coat, then throws away his neckcloth, and
appears ready to reduce his amount of clothing
to the humblest proportions, accompanying his jigs
with frequent shouts of* "Wow!"—*suddenly, however, the* MILITARY *appear upon the scene,* L.U.E., *led*

by MULLIGAN—*the* WOMEN *shriek, the* PEASANTS
look defiant, and the RIVD. PHADRIG *appears to
oscillate between a desire to calm the ruffled feelings of the* NATIVES, *and a wish to knock the*
SOLDIERS *down*)

CAPTAIN CLUTTERBUCK. Which is Miles na Boclish ?
MILES. That's me.
CAPTAIN C. You are my prisoner.
MILES. Niver ! What for ?
CAPTAIN C. You are charged with keeping an illicit
still, with carrying on secret communications with General
Hoche, with being a Whiteboy, with being the private
secretary to Captain Rock, with having killed several
landlords, with having been concerned in the illegal
pawning of a most respectable tithe proctor, and you have
been seen to drop several remarks of an explosive character in an Orange meeting at Cork.

MILES. It's all perfectly thrue; but who can prove it?
MULLIGAN. (*coming forward*) I CAN.

> (*Picture—*EILY *faints in the* SQUIREEN'S *arms,*
> SOLDIERS *seize* MILES, RIVD. PHADRIG *wipes his
> eyes with his shillelagh,* MULLIGAN *grins widely
> with an air of dental triumph,* LADIES *and*
> GENTLEMEN *of the Ballet and Chorus howl as
> the act-drop descends*)

ACT II.

SCENE.—*The Bogs of Mucross; Allen Abbey in the distance, at the right hand the Foil Cave, and the left the
Water Dhuir, the Wakes of Garryowen in the back-
ground. The scene is very dark (the lights being turned
down), and exceedingly lonesome—no other scene being
near it. Slow music as the curtain rises, discovering
MULLIGAN seated, smoking a dhudeen*)

MULLIGAN. Hurrrrh! (*this is a shiver*) It's bitter cold.
I don't half like this job. It's all very well when there's
a lot of fellows with you, but when you're alone it's—it's
—a— (*pauses and then resumes, not being able to find the
word he wanted*) it's *lonely*. I've been a-thinking of my
past life, and all the black deeds I've done, and all the
dreadful blackguard things as I've committed at one time
or the other—especially the other. Let's see: is this
grave long enough for her? (*looks at a newly made grave
in the stage—a trap door of the most mechanical and un-
deceptive nature*) Let me see: she is a head and a half
shorter than me. I'll measure. (*Music—he empties his
pipe against a briar-root at the back of the stage, sneezes
and starts violently at the Irish echo, which says " Bless
you."—he then, tremblingly, and with faltering footsteps,
approaches the trap, and looks down into it shudderingly*)
Hah! it's a dark hole enough. But here goes. (*gets into
the trap, and, lying down, disappears—at the same moment
MILES NA BOCLISH enters from behind the stump of a tree,
R., and, running to the grave, closes down the trap, and
reclines upon it*)

MILES. Hurroo! The murthering omadhaun! I've
settled *your* business, I'm thinking. But, who's this?

The Squireen! (*muffles himself in his whiskey keg and shillelagh*)

Enter SQUIREEN DON'T CAREY, L.

SQUIRE. Hah, yes, this is the spot. My heart revolts at this dark deed, but my father's estate is impoverished, and I cannot wed a peasant's daughter when there is a chance of patching the broken kettle of my fortunes with the tin of Miss Araminta Killiloo, of Castle Killiloo, Connaught. When I spoke of breaking off the match with Eily, she hinted at a breach of promise action. There is but one course then left for me—Mulligan and the tomb? (*observes* MILES, *who is visibly racked with a million conflicting emotions, but, with the ability of a true artiste, contrives to conceal everything he feels*) Hah, Mulligan, you are here. Have you determined to do it at the price?

MILES. I have; but where is the price?

SQUIRE. 'Tis there. (*hands* MILES *a heavy purse—* MILES *pockets it*) And now to conceal myself until the deed is done. (*retires*)

The red cloak of EILY *is apparent on the rocky steps at the back of the stage; the stage is dark, and is only lighted by the roguish, but characteristic, twinkle of* MILES's *right eye.*

MILES. What will I do with all this money? (*pauses, and then, after reflecting, as if struck by a sudden and brilliant notion*) I know. I'll spend it.

EILY. (*who has by this time reached the stage*) Oh dear, it's very dark. I have always noticed that in the night time, and especially when there is no moon, it always *is* dark. (*calls*) I'm here, dear. I say, I'm here. No reply. He is late. What a funny place for an assignation; but clothed in my native modesty and my Colleen Bawn cloak, I can at once resist the shafts of envy and the piercing gusts of the midnight air. (*sneezes twice violently*) I am catching a severe cold, but I am happy.

MILES. (*advancing*) Eily!

EILY. Miles! *you* here! Where is——

MILES. The Squireen? He is a—— (*about to use a strong expression, but correcting himself*) he is a person

unworthy the affection of one of Erin's brightest
daughters. He lured you here in order that you might
be murdered in the coldest possible blood. After having
put you out of the way, he would have led to the
Hymeneal altar the lovely and accomplished daughter of
Colonel Killiloo, of Killiloo Castle, Connaught. Behold
the preliminary announcement of the match in the
Connaught Cricketer's Journal. (*shows* EILY *the paper ;
the moon by this time having risen, she is enabled to peruse
the paragraph touching her lover's perfidy—she comes to a
hard word which she cannot read, and, with a loud shriek,
falls on the stage in a swoon—the* SQUIREEN *comes forward*)

SQUIRE. Villain! I have heard all. Die! (*snaps a
pistol at* MILES—MILES *closes with him—terrific struggle
—*MILES *gets the worst of it, and is knocked down; he
rises to his knees—the* SQUIREEN *has pulled up a small
Irish bog oak tree, and is just about to fell* MILES *to the
earth, when a pistol shot is heard, and the* SQUIREEN *is
struck down—a slight pause*)

O'SHOCK. (*peeping over the high rocks at the left hand*)
It was lucky I managed to hit the right one. Well,
Mister Don't Carey, Esquire, I think I have put the stop
to *your* matrimonial prospects. (*comes down the side of
the rocks with the agility of a Blondin*) Sure, the poor
Eily's fainted. (*bites her finger—she revives*) And the
darlint Miles is all in a swound. (*kicks him—he also
recovers*) Faix, it was lucky I happened to be passing by,
or they'd have all kilt each other, like the Kilkenny cats.

MILES. Eily!

EILY. Miles! (*they embrace—the* MILITARY *and the*
PEASANTS *are heard murmuring* "Follow! follow!")

[Why they should always call out "Follow," on the stage
when in pursuit of anybody is a mystery to the writer of
this drama; but he is the last man to interfere with the stock
customs of the boards, and "Follow" be it, by all means.]

MILES. Ha! the myrmidons of the oppressor come to
drag me back to durance vile. But they shall not. I
will preserve my life if I perish in the attempt.

Enter the MILITARY, *led by* CAPTAIN CLUTTERBUCK, L.U.E.

CAPTAIN C. Miles Na Boclish, I arrest you in——

SQUIRE. (*reviving*) Stay, I can but live two minutes;

let me occupy those hundred and twenty seconds in repent-
ing; and to commence with—here! (*hands out a free
pardon for* MILES, *which he had basely intercepted*) And
to conclude with—there! (*dies*)

MILES. (*to* EILY) Your late lover being dead, there is
nothing wanting to complete your felicity, but——

EILY. (*to Audience*) But the approbation of our kind
friends in front, who, we trust, will never forget the lesson
they have learnt—namely, that virtue gilds the cottage
of the peasant with gold as refined as the manners of the
aristocracy; and love in humble life may prove to the
jealous confirmation strong; and while the heart *may* be
in the Highlands following the soft roe, there *are* homes
without a sewing machine, where a vent-peg is required,
and where you DO double up your perambulators in spite
of a censorious world, and are all the happier for the deed.

ABANDONDINO THE BLOODLESS.

A ROMANTIC DRAMA.

Characters.

ABANDONDINO THE BLOODLESS!
MYSTERIOUS INDIVIDUAL (*in a cloak*).
TWO COCKS (*who crow*).

SCENE.—*An Inn Chamber.*

ABANDONDINO *discovered sitting gloomily in the centre; he is pale and bilious. An old-fashioned kitchen clock on the right of the stage strikes.*

ABAND. (*counting the strokes*) One!—Two!—Three!—Four!—Five!—Six!—Seven!—Eight!—Nine!—Ten!—Eleven!—Twelve!—Thirteen!—Fourteen!—Humph! it will soon be daybreak. For three years and a quarter no traveller has put up at my hostelry. With difficulty, therefore, can I squeeze a profit from my annual returns. The house, I fear me, has an evil name. Seven poor travellers who stayed here during the great race week of five years since, when Maccaroni ran a dead heat with Cardinal Wiseman, and both won by eight necks—ever since then, I say, when the seven customers came in and

C

did *not* go out again, slander's venomed breath has been
a going on at me awful.   It's fearful to be alone and
know what I know—but what is this, Abandondino—a
tear? luckily it fell in the spittoon.   Conscience, get out!
(*Music—a knock*)

ABAND. Who's there?
VOICE. Me!
ABAND. Ha! that is the smith's vice! come in.
(*opens door*)

Enter MYSTERIOUS INDIVIDUAL, *in a cloak*, L.

INDIVIDUAL. I would sleep here! There is gold! Call
me at half-past four in the afternoon of next Friday week.

ABAND. (*aside, after several strong spasms*) Next Friday week! the fatal day on which I killed my wife and
packed off my infant son and hare in a game hamper,
directing it to the Chancellor of Exchequer on account of
unpaid Income-tax (*after a struggle with himself, turns—
more pale and bilious if possible than before—to* INDIVIDUAL)
You—you cannot sleep here.

INDIVIDUAL. (*sitting* C.) I will.   (*sleeps*)

ABAND. How sudden is the slumbering of the innocent.

INDIVIDUAL. (*reviving suddenly*) Oh, by the way, my
luggage is without, consisting of a couple of pen wipers
and a tooth brush.   Fetch them.

ABAND. (*aside, with malignity*) 'Twas ever thus from
childhood's hour; but I will humour him.   *Exit*, R.

INDIVIDUAL. (*looking round*) Time indeed works won-
ders, and *honi soit qui mal y pense*; but I anticipate.

ABANDONDINO *returns with box*, R.

ABAND. Why travel with this? (*holding up the tooth brush*) I keep one for the use of all my customers.

INDIVIDUAL. Varlet, the bloom is on the rye, and let the best man win.

ABAND. Enough, I am answered.

INDIVIDUAL. Remember, next Friday week, at half-past four. (*sleeps*)

ABAND. The day! the hour! He sleeps. (*in a hoarse whisper, and exhibiting as many teeth as possible*) He must never WAKE! (*creeps stealthily up to him and bawls with all his might in his ear*) Boohoo! Hurryaba-goolabah! (*pause*)

INDIVIDUAL. (*in his sleep*) Some one whispered my mother's name.

ABAND. Poor boy. And yet he must die. (*goes to clock, opens it, and produces an enormous horse pistol*) This pistol is loaded with powder, several slugs, and a couple of ordinary snails. What is this feeling that comes over me and chills me to the marrow-bone? Pshaw! also Tush! likewise Pish! not mention Bosh! (*points the pistol at* INDIVIDUAL) One, Two—(*a loud crow is heard,* ABANDONDINO *drops the pistol*)

The rooster's toll'd the knell of parting night,
'Tis he, my lord, the burly British cock,
The cock crows sal-volatile to the morn.

INDIVIDUAL. (*awakes*) Where is my box?

ABAND. There.

INDIVIDUAL. It contains a change of linen and the certificate of my birth.

ABAND. His loose kit, and his stiff-kit—oh, agony, you *have* a strawberry pottle on your middle temple?

INDIVIDUAL. Yes, a hautboy.

ABAND. Hautboy! Ho, boy, you are *my* boy!

INDIVIDUAL. And you—you—if I am your son, there can be but one conclusion—namely, that *you* are my——

ABAND. Father. Yes. Embrace me! (*embrace—the two roosters appear at window and crow*) Nothing but the approbation of our kind friends is now necessary.

INDIVIDUAL. Here are our hands—join but yours, then (*holding out his luggage*) Box——

ABAND. (*pointing the roosters*) And Cocks——
BOTH. Are satisfied.

Curtain.

VILLAGE VIRTUE;

OR,

THE LIBERTINE LORD AND THE DAMSEL OF DAISY FARM.

A DOMESTIC DRAMA OF THRILLING INTEREST.

Characters.

FARMER FOURACRES (*of the Daisy Farm*).
LORD LEVERET (*his Landlord, a Roué, Libertine, and Gambler*).
HODGE (*a young Peasant*).
LAURA. (*the Damsel of Daisy Farm*).

SCENE.—*A Cornfield. Gate* R.

VILLAGERS *carousing. The last load has just been carted, and* FARMER FOURACRES *in top boots, and with a whip, the inevitable accompaniments of stage agricultural parents, stands* L., *and beer.*

Opening Chorus of PEASANTS.
Oh, such a load
We never know'd;
No, such a load
We never know'd.

Solo by tenor CHORUS SINGER (*with a moustache*)

The jolly, jolly rain
Has raised the golden grain,
The go-o-o-o-lden gra ·ain.
 Fill high the flowing can,
And drink to the wealth
And continual health
 Of that most respectable man,
Farmer Fouracres,
Farmer Fou-u-r-a-acres ;
 For (*long cadence*) he's a jolly good fellow,
(*repeated twice*)
 And—

ALL. So say all of us !

(PEASANTS *hurrah, and take long draughts of nothing whatever out of their tin mugs, which in the enthusiasm of the chorus, they have frequently held sideways and occasionally upside down*)

FARMER. Lads, I thank'ee. There's not a man or woman in my employ that I don't love better than my own children. And now let's go whoam. The glorious luminary of day is a shutting up, and night is a casting of her shadows around.

(*the music is repeated, and the* PEASANTS *take up the chorus, mugs, &c., and go off,* R. *and* L.)

FARMER. (*solus*) Happy fellows, they know no cares. They have all large families with tremendous teeth, and their wages average three and sixpence a week. Well may Old England glory in her peasant sons. But my mind misgives me about my Laura, my child, the prop of my declining years. She comes. (*Music*)

Enter LAURA, R.

LAURA. Dearest father !
FARMER. Prop of. my declining years !
LAURA. Do not chide your daughter if she appears too bold—but the tea is ready.
FARMER. Daughter—prop. Laura there are moments when tea is unattractive, when bread and butter, however

thick, is apt to pall, and the fragrant watercress loses its accustomed charm.

LAURA. Father, what mean these wild and haggard words? There is an unsteady tremor in your eye. You You have some secret to communicate. Oh, by the memory of my grandmother, (FARMER *is strongly agitated and drops several H's*) tell me what it is. (*kneels, and flings her hair back wildly*)

FARMER. Prop of my declining years, the Squire— (LAURA *shrinks visibly*) the Squire, who is also the lieutenant of the county, likewise member for the borough, not to mention lord of the manor, to say nothing of being my landlord—Lord Leveret—has made me an offer for your hand.

LAURA. Forgive me, father.

FARMER. Never! what have you done?

LAURA. I cannot say. My soul shrinks from your gaze. I have done wrong — (*guggle*) — very—(*guggle*)—very wrong.

FARMER. Have you neglected to milk the cows? Say, have you left them to Giles, Stephen, or—or any udder man?

LAURA. No—no!

FARMER. Hah, then—but no, impossible—and yet—not so—because—or even—why not—just so—precisely— nevertheless it could scarcely be—oh, 'orror! (*sits down*, R., *on his luck*)

LAURA. Yes, father, you have guessed rightly.

FARMER. You have jilted Hodge!

LAURA. Forgive me!

FARMER. And for——

LAURA. Lord Leveret!

FARMER. (*after a lengthy but internal paroxysm*) Oh!

LAURA. He saw me—loved me. He has promised me wealth, position, a house in Park-lane, seven carriages, footmen with sensation calves, boxes at both operas, sub-scription to Mudie's, pin-money, and——

HODGE *rushing on*, R. U. E.

HODGE. What do I hear! False? Oh, cockatrice! (*punches his own head severely*)

FARMER. (*with the tearfulness of despair*) Young man,

don't call my daughter a cockatrice. The father of a cockatrice must be an *old* cockatrice, and such an appellation at the present moment would be too much for my white hairs. (*weeps*)

HODGE. I will not upbraid you, Laura. Marry Lord Leveret. Be happy in your gilded home. May your dwelling be a Paradise of bliss, untainted with the odour of the corduroys that once you loved. No word of anger or reproach shall pass my lips. You nasty, ugly, good-for-nothing baggage, you ought to be put on bread and water and well whipped.

LAURA. Oh, Hodge! dear Hodge! these kind and loving words cut me to the quick. I cannot endure this pitying gentleness. Revile me! spurn me with your indignant blucher, but do not—a—do not—a—speak ke—yindly—a—to me. (*covers her face with her hand—soft music, through which* HODGE *speaks*)

HODGE. This is no place for me. I shall emigrate. In the wild excitement of Margate I may hope to drown all recollections of my early sorrow! Farewell!

(*rushes off,* L.)

LAURA. Gone! fled! decamped! Oh, wretched Laura! open earth, and swallow me, for indeed, indeed, I am—a—very, very wretched. (*feeling flat, falls so*)

FARMER. This is indeed a wretched sight for a farmer. But what is this, Ralph Fouracres,—tears? with your best waistcoat on too? never! Laura, your father goes to his tea, but more, much more, in sorrow than in anger.

Music—Exit FARMER FOURACRES, R.

Enter Lord Leveret, *elevated,* l.

Lord L. Wheresh Laura? Tish the pointed splot she
greed to meet mer. Whatsh shignal? Oh, ha, *variety*!
N'ansher. Try 'gain, *variety*! Whatsh thish? (*sees*
Laura) Hah! Laura dead! (*chord—his Lordship
becomes sober immediately*) What dastard has done this?
My Laura, awake; it is your Leveret. (*kneels and raises
her in his arms*)

Laura. Where am I?

Lord L. Hee-ar. In the arr-ums of—a—Leveret.

Laura. Leveret! Oh, I pant for hare—give it me. (*pants*)

Lord L. (*aside*) A golden opportunity—she faints and
cannot resist. I will bear her away, far, far from here.
(*raises her in his arms*) Come, Laura, to bliss and Belinda
Cottages.

Laura. (*disengaging herself from him*) What words
are these? Oh, Leveret, my mind misgives me. You
would take advantage of the innocent, and bring a parent's
Welsh wig with sorrow to the Union.

Lord L. Bah, I know no union but ours; St. George's,
Hanover——

Laura. *Square?*

Lord L. I ser-ware it.

Laura. No, no. I have been imprudent, but not guilty;
it is not too late to retrace my steps; I will return to my
father. If I have a weakness, it's muffins, which something whispers to my heart are rapidly disappearing before
a blighted but hungry parent—unhand me!

LORD L. If you go to tea, it will be over my mangled a—corpse.

LAURA. So be it then; it is war to the knife, is it? Behold! "The young woman's best companion."

                (*produces a large horse pistol*)

LORD L. (*aside*) Ha! then I must dissemble,

                (*retires to the back and dissembles*)

LAURA. Oh, I am racked with a million emotions.

LORD L. (*comes down*) Laura, I cannot resist my fate, come on. (LAURA *and* LEVERET *struggle—the pistol falls*)

Enter HODGE, L.; *he knocks down* LEVERET; LEVERET *rises —fierce struggle—*HODGE *is felled to the earth, and* LEVERET *is escaping, when* FARMER FOURACRES *enters, R., and seizing the pistol, fires at* LEVERET—*the pistol snaps without going off, and* LEVERET *falls wounded.*

LEVERET. Ha! ha! you thought to kill me; but, ha! ha! the bullet has not reached its mark. (*faints*)

FARMER. What have I done?

HODGE. See, he breathes! here is a hole in his coat; but see, his heart is protected by layers of parchment.

LEVERET. (*struggling*) Ha! do not touch that—it is private.

HODGE. (*tearing a large deed from* LEVERET's *breast*) What's this? a will! my name on it, too! What does it mean?

LEVERET. The icy film of death is on my brow, and his pallid finger in my eye—why not confess all? Hodge, you—*you* are the rightful heir. I was old in crime e'en when but an infant in months. I was your foster-brother; in the absence of the nurse—my mother—I crept into your cradle, having previously flung you out. Forgive me, for I was but two months old, and youth will have its fling.—You—you are the real Lord Leveret, and I——

       (*attempts to die, but is prevented by two* POLICEMEN, *who enter, L., and handcuff him*)

LAURA. Hodge—that is—my Lord——

HODGE. Lord fiddlesticks! I am Hodge—the Hodge of your youthful love. (*they embrace*)

FARMER. (*to audience*) And, ladies and gentlemen, you will perhaps permit a fond parent to observe— "What's the Hodge so long as you're 'appy?"

Curtain.

THE
MENDACIOUS MARINER;

OR,

PRETTY POLL OF PORTSEA AND THE CAPTAIN WITH HIS WHISKERS.

A MORE THAN USUALLY NAUTICAL DRAMA.

Characters.

CAPTAIN CAPSTAN (*of H.M.S. Thunder Bomb*).
LIEUTENANT LEE SCUPPER (*First Lieutenant of same*).
SECOND LIEUTENANT.
WILLIAM TAYLOR (*Tailor, of Portsea*).
MARY.

ACT I.

SCENE.—*Portsmouth Hard.*

Enter WILLIAM TAYLOR, *with his arm round the waist of*
MARY, L.

WILLIAM. Yes, Mary, to-morrow is to be the happy day. Will you, under the circumstances, excuse me for remarking—Oh, rapture!

MARY. Yes, dear William. Till I met you my heart was free, so was my manners. But you, dear William, have shown me that life is but a summer's day; and also that there is a flower that bloometh. These truths sunk deeply into my heart. I now know how false are the vows and ringlets of a hollow world. I am fully aware of the baseness and villany of everything and everybody, and I am—a—happy.

WILLIAM. Bless you, my blue-eyed artless one. But hark! I hear the measured tread of intoxicated sailors. We will retire. (*runs away, but is stopped by sudden entrance of* LIEUTENANT LEE SCUPPER *and* SAILORS, R.)

MARY. The pressgang! Ha! my sex protects me.

LIEUTEN. Well, reef my binnacle, and porthole my sternsail larboard, if here isn't as tight a looking lad for His Majesty's frigate the *Thunder Bomb* as ever weakened his grog with whimpering after his grandmother, or danced the sailor's hornpipe to the tune of fifty lashes.

MARY. (*kneeling to* LIEUTENANT) Spare him; his lungs are weak!

WILLIAM. (*tearfully*) So are his knees.

LIEUTEN. (*relenting for the moment*) This is affecting. It is many a year since the tear of pity has moistened the weather-beaten cheeks of old Lee Scupper. But, pshaw! the Fleet requires manning. (*to* MEN) Seize him!

WILLIAM. Beware! (MEN *hang back*) Beware, I say. I am a desperate man. Tempt me not too far, or I *may* run away. (MEN *tremble visibly*)

LIEUTEN. (*to his* MEN) Cowards! What, do I not see among ye faces scorched by the powder of a thousand fights? Are there not those in your ranks who carry in your bodies twenty-four pound shots, the result of too reckless daring; and yet afraid to tackle him? I am aware the odds are overwhelming, but your king and country demand it, and I will blow out the brains of the first man who doesn't seize the lubber. (*he produces a horse pistol and levels it at his* MEN, *who immediately rush upon* WILLIAM *and secure him*)

MARY. (*aside*) What shall I do? Shall I rush down to the railway station, and like a second Ravina, madly fire the train? No, 'twould be better to stay and blow them up upon the spot. (*to* LIEUTENANT) Dastard! R-r-r-uffian! Take yon trembling youth at your peril. Remember, I vow (and the vow is registered; so, pro-vincial managers, beware!) to have revenge!

LIEUTEN. Away with him!

WILLIAM. (*distinctly audible through the wild shrieks of*

MARY, *the savage shouts of the* SAILORS, *the thunders of a sudden storm, and the superhuman efforts of the orchestra*) Farewell—my—my (*relapsing into poetry and tears*)—my "trim built wherry."

Act-drop descends on a harrowing spectacle·

ACT II.

SCENE.—*The Deck of H.M.S. Thunder Bomb. Everything is all ataunto (whatever that may be), and the* SAILORS *are pulling up the anchor, or letting it down or doing something with it (or something else), which the more nautical among the audience will understand and appreciate.*

Chorus of Ancient and Modern Mariners.

The Brine! the Brine! the Brine!
They may talk of the river Tyne,
Of the Thames and the Lea also,
Where the stormy winds *don't* blow;
But the Brine! the Brine! the Brine!
For auld lang syne, lang syne, lang syne,
Is better by far,
Ha! ha! ha! har!
With a yeo, heave ho,
And away we go,
Before the breeze,
Through the roaring seas,
When the stormy wind do, do blow;
With a yeo, heave ho, heave ho, heave ho,
Over the billows and over the brine,
As jolly as gentlefolk over their wine.
The jolly, jolly Bri-i-i-ne!

(*all the* SAILORS, *at the conclusion of the Chorus, burst into fits of laughter, and push and knock each other about in the hilarity of the moment. This is conventional and most important*)

1st SAILOR. (*taking an observation*) Latitude forty-six in the shade by W.C.

2ND SAILOR. (*reefing a topsail*) Yeo-ho-o-o!

3RD SAILOR. (*taking soundings*) By the mark two hundred and sixteen.

4TH SAILOR. (*hitching*) Shiver my timbers!

5TH SAILOR. (*scratching*) Ah!

YOUTHFUL MIDSHIPMAN. (*speaking to the* MAN *at the wheel*) Are we off Gravesend yet? (YOUTHFUL MIDSHIP-MAN *is immediately placed in irons*)

Enter up the companion-ladder the CAPTAIN WITH THE WHISKERS, LIEUTENANT LEE SCUPPER, *and the* " MYSTERIOUS MARINER."

CAPTAIN. Ha! ha!

LIEUTENANT. (*in a fawning spirit of toadyism*) Very good! just your way—will have your joke.

MYST. MAR. Well, shiver my maintop gallant spritsail moorings! I can't see the captain's joke.

CAPTAIN. Ha, insubordination! and so soon. Young man, I like your bold demeanour, your frank behaviour. The way in which you helped yourself to the best bits of the beef at my table, and coolly took my glass of champagne from under my nose and drank it off, won an old sailor's heart. There is something mysterious about you. Who are you?

LIEUTENANT. (*becoming gradually livid with jealousy*) Ah! that's what *I* want to know. Look at the white hands of the new sailor. Do you not suspect?

CAPTAIN. Lee Scupper, suspicion ever haunts the guilty mind. Beware, my lad, of jealousy; an honest man is worth two in the bush—more. (*winks*)

LIEUTENANT. (*cowering, and aside*) Humph! but a day *will* come. (*retires within himself, and pulls down the blinds*)

MYST. MAR. I am anxious to conceal my name and station. I was a volunteer; do not press me.

Enter SECOND LIEUTENANT, *who is a most elegant young man.*

2ND LIEUTENANT. Far be it from me, captain, to interrupt a *tête-à-tête:* but, if I may be excused for

mentioning it, I rather think we are about six inches off
a French line-of-battle ship, the crew of which are in the
act of boarding. As your inferior officer, I considered it
my painful duty to inform you of this. If I have acted
wrongly, you will confer an obligation upon me by taking
my life.

CAPTAIN. (*amazed*) Enemy! French! boarding! (*leans
against something or other, and gently relapses into
second childhood*)

MYST. MAR. (*suddenly taking the command of the
vessel*) Ho, here! Reef everything! Let go your
taffrail halyards! Splice all main-braces! Point everything that'll go off at the enemy. Now then, take the
word from me—fire!

> (*dreadful scene of havoc—the two vessels come up
> against each other with a bang—general encounter
> —MYSTERIOUS MARINER is always in the thick,
> and LEE SCUPPER always in the thin, of the fray—
> CAPTAIN CAPSTAN descends at the first shot to his
> cabin, being undesirous of sacrificing his valuable
> life—the enemy strike, and everything is settled in
> favour of the English vessel, when a concluding
> shot from the French frigate knocks off the sailor's
> hat of the MYSTERIOUS MARINER, and his—that is
> —HER "back hair" comes down, to the grief and
> astonishment of the crew*)

CAPTAIN. (*having boldly ascended the deck on hearing of
the conclusion of the fight*) What do I see? A woman!

LIEUTENANT. (*whose jealousy becomes immediately merged in admiration*) Ha! she shall be mine—a. (*retires to back and forms a deep design*)

MARY. (*for* SHE *is the Mysterious Mariner*) Yes.; as you have discovered the fact, concealment is unworthy a British female. I have come out in search of my own true lover, W. Taylor, able-bodied seaman.

CAPTAIN. Maiden, if I may be allowed to call you so, your Taylor is false. He is away on leave, and is "carrying on," if I may be permitted the expression, with a lady to whom, I believe, he is shortly to be united. The smoke has cleared away, and if you will look through my telescope, you will distinctly perceive the features of your faithless Taylor walking on the shore, arm-in-arm with what, under the circumstances, I think I am justified in denominating a "creature."

MARY. (*after taking a sight at the distant form of* TAYLOR, *who* IS *walking on the beach with a* LADY) Give me a sword and pistol. (*the entire* CREW *rush to obey her command*)

(*after selecting a cream-coloured Colt*) 'Tis well! (*takes aim at* TAYLOR, *and fires*) Dead! (*sighs*) Well, *that's* off my mind!

LIEUTENANT. Noble, daring girl, will you accept my hand?

CAPTAIN. Lieutenant Lee Scupper, consider yourself under arrest; *I* shall marry this lady. (*to* CRW) Take the *late* Lieutenant, and load him with te heaviest irons

D

you can find, with as many "flat" and "Italian" ones as
possible, and place in him the deepest dungeon, beneath
the dampest moat of the first castle we come across.
Through the fitful moaning of the wind, the gasps of the
faithless Taylor, who is dying very hard upon the shingle,
are distinctly audible to the naked ear; what, then, is
there wanting to complete the felicity of the Captain's
wife—the new First Lieutenant of the gallant Thunder
Bomb?

(CREW *hurrah*—LEE SCUPPER, *on hearing that he is
superseded, drops a more than usual manly tear,
which is immediately swabbed up by the* SECOND
LIEUTENANT)

MARY. (*coming forward archly—provincial actresses
are informed that unless they are " arch" in this situation,
the entire effect will be marred*) WHAT is there wanting
to complete her felicity, you naughty, naughty hubby?
(*patting the decided cheek of the* CAPTAIN) Why, the
approbation of our key-ind friends, who, let us hope, will
not entirely forget the fate of the Mendacious Mariner,
the trials of Poll of Portsea, and the gallant conduct of
the Captain with the Whiskers. (*the* CREW *cheer—land
appears on the lee-bow—a rainbow spans the back of the
scene—the enemy's vessel blows up, and* LIEUTENANT LEE
SCUPPER *expires from the effect of a slow poison, as the
curtain descends rapidly*)

THE WILD WOLF OF TARTARY;

OR,

THE EMPTY KHAN AND THE KHURDISH CONSPIRATORS.

A GRAND EQUESTRIAN DRAMATIC SPECTACLE.

Characters.

Assid (*the Tartaric Khan*).	2ND CONSPIRATOR.
AL KALI (*his enemy*).	3RD CONSPIRATOR.
1ST CONSPIRATOR.	COURTIERS, &c.

SCENE.—*The Steppes of Tartary.*

Enter THREE KURDISH CONSPIRATORS *at different entrances.*

1ST CON. The Khan of Tartary is——

2ND CON. Worse! I consider him——

3RD CON. Why mince matters? It is universally admitted he——

1ST CON. He must not live.

2ND CON. Certainly not; it is for the interests of the State, and the general community that he should die. That being determined upon, it simply waits for us to settle *when*.

3RD CON. At once—on this spot. (*indicates a particular place on the stage, which is inspected and approved of by* 1ST *and* 2ND CONSPIRATORS)

1ST CON. But see—he comes!

2ND CON. Base tyrant; he is *always* coming.

3RD CON. (*with grim intensity*) But he will soon be going!

1ST CON. Muffle me, night, awhile. (*retires to be muffled,* R.)

2ND CON. " Shades of evening close not o'er us."

(*retires,* L.)

3RD CON. (*to audience*) They think I am with them; but—— Ha, ha! no matter.

(*Music.*—3RD CONSPIRATOR *winks twice; produces handcuffs, kisses them with fervour, and hides*

D 2

them again—a sudden and tremendous burst of noisy martial music, in which there is more than the ordinary amount of cymbal—after a few bars of a loud military march, the music ceases)

3RD CON. (*after having thrown himself on the stage and listened with his ear close to the boards*) Hah! surely I cannot be mistaken ; there is a sound of music! (*tremendous solo on the ophecleide*) At first I took it for the soft sigh of the wind, or the plaintive wail of the wood violet. However, repetition convinces me it is the Imperial band of the Tartarian Khan; he whose life— but I anticipate. My two companions have gone different ways; I will go up the Steppes until I have arrived sufficiently high to see them, and then—ha! ha! to keep an eye on both. (*goes off stealthily—march continued*)

GRAND PROCESSION.

Enter the Pioneer Forte, *followed by* Dancing Dervishes
—*then* Four Tartar Emetics (*or private physicians to
the Khan*)—*then the Prime Minister* Tar-Tar Samivel,
in his robes of office—*then an* Array of Royal
Academicians, *drawn in a handsome carte de visite or
morning-call coach*—*then the* Imperial Dramatic Company of Cossacks, *who of co-sacks so admirably*—
then several Plum Tartars, *being the wealthiest men
of the kingdom, some of them being Sir-cash-'uns*—
following these come the Khan's Corps de Ballet,
composed of the Cream of Tartar Dancers—*and
then the* Khan *in a splendid carriage of state*—Tag
Rag *and* Roberttail *in (very) ordinary to the Khan*—
the Crowd *throw up their caps, and wave their hand-
kerchiefs, whilst the* Musicians *flourish their trumpets*)

Khan. (*coming down*) Bless you, my children!

1ST COURTIER. What eloquence!

2ND COURTIER. And what brevity!

3RD COURTIER. (*a wag*) Which is the soul of wit. (*all laugh, in which the* COURT *joins*)

KHAN. But where is Al Kali, my nephew?

Enter AL KALI, R.   *He is sulky and defiant.*

KHAN. Al Kali, I hope I see you.

ALI. Khan, I scorn and spit upon ye! Who killed my father, mother, two sisters, three brothers, seven servants, house, horse, and pony-chaise? Who devas-tated my home, upset my Lares and Penates, blighted the joy of my household, and set his cruel foot upon the domestic beetle of my hearth stone? Echo answers, "Which it's the Khan."

KHAN. Echo not only speaks bad grammar, but lies in her throat. (*draws his rifle, and cocks his sceptre*) Thus doth Assid Khan punish those who rebel against his authority. (*selects a soft spot on the head of* AL KALI, *and with one blow fells him to the earth*)

KHAN. And now we will proceed upon our journey.

(*lively music—the Procession wends its way over the Steppes,* R. U. E., *leaving the prostrate nephew of the* KHAN *in the centre of the stage, pale and determined*)

AL KALI. Can it be? or is it all a hideous dream? A blow! and delivered with a fatal steadiness of aim upon the one bald oasis in my Desert of Sa-hairer! I have endured much, but *now*—— (*whistles*)

Enter simultaneously the THREE CONSPIRATORS.

'Tis well! not a moment must be lost in securing the crown of the kingdom, and our own heads; a second's delay may be fatal. A short pause for a glee, and then to horse.

Glee—the 3RD CONSPIRATOR *pretending to join in, but, for motives of his own, which will transpire in the sequel, not doing so.*

The Wolf of the Steppes is a terrible thing,
It flies o'er the earth with a light'ning wing;
Oh, beware! oh, beware! when there's no one by,
Of the feverish flash in that animal's eye;

For it winks and it blinks with a hateful sneer,
And its yell is doom in the traveller's ear;
And its terrible teeth are all bared to the gums,
And it's equal to any nutrition that comes
In the way of the Wolf—in the dead of the night;
For he's got a peculiar sort of a bite;
And he's always as hungry as hungry can be
Is the Wolf of the Steppes.

3RD CON. (*cutting in*)   Which are not in Step-*nce*.

(*indignation on the part of the two other* CON-
SPIRATORS, *and sneer of contempt from* AL KALI—
*the chorus is then repeated pianissimo, and to the
final strains of the music, the* TWO CONSPIRATORS
and AL KALI *slink off*, R.—*the* 3RD CONSPIRATOR
is left on the stage)

3RD CON. Since I was an infant, and took delight in
tinselling Skelt's penny characters, I have always delighted
in foiling villains. Here comes the Khan! More partial
to the charms of virtuous solitude than the pomp and
parade of regal splendour, he has come to this lone spot
to cool himself. Humph!

Enter the KHAN, *reflectively*, R. U. E.

KHAN. Where is my long-lost son? Ah! where is he?
Years have rolled by, but he has never returned. And
yet I was never cruel to him; never spoke one harsh
word to him. Perhaps—indeed more than likely—he is
dead. How many thousand of my poorer subjects are at
this hour asleep! *I* have not slept since my boy left his
home. It is some years now. Ya-a-a-h! (*yawns*) I feel
somewhat drowsy. (*lies down*) "Uneasy lies the head
that wears a crown." (*takes off his crown, and wrapping
it in his ermine robe, makes an extemporaneous pillow
of it*) How sweet it is to quit the hubbub of the court for
the calm seclusion of solitude! May the present moment
be the worst of our lives. (*sleeps*)

3RD CON. (*gazing on the sleeping form of the* KHAN)
Humph! yes, ah, indeed; just so, of course; and yet
why? but it always was so; and all things considered—
why not? (*weeps copiously*)

Enter the WILD WOLF OF TARTARY, *hungry*, L. U. E.

3RD CON. What do I see? The Volpas! The Wild Wolf! The terror of the country! What is to be done?

(*the* WILD WOLF *walks round the* KHAN, *evidently with the object of selecting a soft place to begin upon*)

KHAN. (*in his sleep*) My son, my Waldemar, my boy! If he will return to his agonised parent, all shall be forgiven. No cards. Friends will please accept this intimation. P.P.C., and I may add R.V.S.V.P. For characters see small bills. (*again sleeps*)

3RD CON. (*to* WILD WOLF) Hoosh! (*shakes his fist at him*)

WILD WOLF. Howowowgrrrbullwrhow!

3RD CON. Ha! I have my two revolvers. I will fire at him, or perish in the attempt. (*fires the twelve barrels—misses each time—draws his sword*) This is to thy heart-a! (*runs the* WILD WOLF *through; the blade having passed through the body of the* WOLF, *grazes the calf of the sleeping Monarch—he rises*)

KHAN. What! Treachery! (*springs the Imperial rattle*)

Enter, on horseback, the SUITE—1ST *and* 2ND CONSPIRATORS *very prominent—* AL KALI *likewise forward.*

KHAN. Assassination! Seize the slave!

AL KALI. Never! He was but doing my bidding. He is in my pay; concealment is no longer of any avail. I must have the crown. Khan, you're an old idiot. The people are with me. Are you not, people? (*no reply from the people*) Yes; I see your hearts are too full for words. (*to* KHAN) Die! (*he thrusts at the* KHAN—*the blade is parried by* 3RD CONSPIRATOR, *who appears in the simple but effective uniform of the Tartarian Detective—before* AL KALI *can resist, the quondam conspirator handcuffs him—consternation*) Sold again!

DETECTIVE. (*pocketing the reward which has been handed him by the* FIRST LORD OF THE TREASURY) And got the money.

KHAN. (*to* DETECTIVE) You have preserved my life;

but something tells me you are more near and dear to me than that uniform would suggest. You are——

DETECTIVE. Do not press me, your Majesty. Seek not to know who I am.

KHAN. (*greatly agitated*) You had a father?

DETECTIVE. I admit it.

KHAN. (*more agitated than ever*) I had a son. (*the* COURTIERS, TROOPS, PHYSICIANS, *and* SUPERNUMERARIES *become painfully interested*) Tell me—in pity, tell me—are you my son?

DETECTIVE. Hush! (*leads the* KHAN *forward with a great air of mystery*) I would rather have perished in a foreign land than have divulged this dreadful secret, but——

KHAN. Proceed—this suspense is awful! *Are* you my son?

DETECTIVE. No, your Majesty; I am NOT.

KHAN. Oh, indeed. (*reflects for some time, and then waking up to the necessity for action, smilingly observes*) Then there is nothing left me but to ask our kind friends to overlook the many failings of the Wild Wolf of Tartary, the Empty Khan, and the Three Kurdish Conspirators. (*general discharge of artillery—most of the men returning to their families—as the curtain descends with rapid strides*)

THE

WAYSIDE WIOLETS;

OR,

THE GIPSY GIRL AND THE GUILTY CONSCIENCE.

Characters.

DITANTIPALPITI (*Chief of the Zingari, known in his tribe as Il Dufferio, or, "The Duffer."*)

LEONARD DALTON.

SIR RUBY GLENGORE (*A Gambler and a Roué*).

SULKI (*a Zingaro*).

SCENE.—*A Gipsy Encampment in a bye-lane on the estate of Sir Ruby Glencore. Several tents are pitched by the MALE GIPSIES and caught by the FEMALES. The donkeys are feeding at the roadside, with contentment evident on their peaceful browse. A caravan, left in care of ANN (an old gipsy woman) at the back. The supper is preparing, and a contract must be entered into with " Williams's Boiled Beef Establishment," or some other dining rooms, for the odour of a savoury stew, to be wafted through the house during the entire scene, after Mr. Rimmel's style of scenting, in order to give a life-like reality to the representation.*

Gipsy Chorus.

Who so happy, who so free
As the gip gip-gip, as the gip-gip-see?

Over the meadows, over the lea,
Under the shade of the greenwood-tree,
Merrily, Merrily, Merrily, we
Live—Ha, Ha, Ha! Ho, Ho, Ho! He, He, Hee!
The gallant, the gay, and the bold Romance,
Blithe and as free as the wild honey-bee;
And as our brethren the dark Zingari;
Happy must be every swarthy gipsee.

(they enter their tents and disappear)

Enter DITANTIPALPITI, *the Chief of the Zingari*, L.

DITAN. May my heaviest hatred, my most ponderous
detestation, my most scorching contempt, my sarcastic-est
sneers, light on the chilling land on which I now place my
foreign foot! Ever since I left the blue skies of the beloved
South, where the grape-juice dances in the sparkling
sunlight of the sapphire sea; where the chamois bounds
along the pebbly promontory overlooking the burning
lava of the volcanic agency to which my long-lost son, I
hear, is secretary—ever since I bid farewell to the beautiful clime where the dusky natives open without knives
and shrink into their shells at the merest suggestion of the
vinegar of a colder land—ever since I departed from the
tents of that distant people—so distant, in fact, that at
last they wouldn't recognise me—ever since I came to
shiver in this vile country where I am allowed to do
what I please and am never interfered with (confusion
seize it!)—ever since, I say, I have been in England, I
have been racked with a million emotions. And why?
Ha! ha! *Why?* That's the ticket.

Enter LINDA, *his daughter*, R., *with a tambourine (indispensable) and a bounding pirouette.*

DITAN. Daughter of a despised and branded race, how
are you?

LINDA. Father of a small but highly-intellectual family,
I'm bobbish.

DITAN. *Bobbish.* How soon have you picked up the
unmellifluous colloquialisms of this guttural clime. My
child, it is time that you should wed.

LINDA. (*looking at her watch*) My dear father, it is scarcely ten o'clock.

DITAN. This equivocation, Linda, is unworthy. Sulki loves you, and would marry you.

LINDA. Oh, father, I love him not; indeed, I hate and despise him. It is true he has followed me from the sunny clime in which he was nurtured—

DITAN. Yes, daughter; followed you to this frosty land, and he has never been without a cold in his head since he put his foot upon the shivering shores of England. But what is catarrh to true love? He has purchased the insular pocket-handkerchief, and though it must be admitted he has acquired a snuffle which has become chronic, his heart is still the same. He is thine, ever thine.

LINDA. (*after a tearful pause*) Oh, bother!

DITAN. I fear me some ruddy youth amongst the tribe we have joined has stolen your affections. Ha! is't so?

LINDA. (*starting, but almost immediately coming back again*) What makes you think so?

SULKI, *a young Zingaro*, L., *enters and listens.*

DITAN. With the exception of four hearty meals a day, you eat scarcely anything. You drop off to sleep at night and seldom wake until late in the morning; you grow plumper every hour; you sing and dance when there is no occasion; all these symptoms tell a watchful parent that the cankerworm is gnawing at your inmost feelings. What is your objection to Sulki?

LINDA. I love—another. (DITANTIPALPITI *and* SULKI *draw large knives simultaneously*)

SULKI. Tell me who he is, and if he is asleep in his tent, regardless of the consequences, I will kill him before he has time to awake.

DITAN. My own brave lad! But do not be impulsive. Listen.

LINDA. He who has wooed and won me is no gipsy. I should think not indeed!

DITAN. Is he——

SULKI. Or is he——

LINDA. I don't know what either of you mean, but he isn't.

DITAN. Is he rich?

·LINDA. I have never cared to inquire, but I have made it my business to find out that he is an only orphan child, whose brothers and sisters are all provided for and whose parents are in the enjoyment of a snug property; he is down in his uncle german's will for a reversion of the family peerage, which has been extinct for some generations; he keeps two hunters, one jewelled and double-cased; he subscribes to a pack of cards, and boldly mounted on his Arab steed, has been frequently detected scouring his front door-steps; he is so fond of practical jokes that he has on more than one occasion been observed attempting to "take in" the milk; he is, all my fancy painted him, and more than Herbert Watkins photographed him; he is lovely, he is divine, and (*in a cart-horse whisper*) *he is there!* (*points to a tent at the back*)

SULKI. Is he asleep? and is he armed?

LINDA. He is wide awake, and has two arms, with fists at the end of them.

SULKI. I can afford to despise him. (*runs away*)

DITAN. Produce your admirer. Let me see if he will brave the indignant glances of an outraged parent.

(LINDA *whistles, and* LEONARD DALTON *appears,* R.)

DITAN. (*surveying him from the boots to the hat, and then down again*) Well, stripling, ye show some hardiness in entering the tents of a powerful tribe alone, and——

LEONARD. On a hot night—precisely, I *do;* to endure the odours of stew and corduroy combined, in the month of July, one requires a constitution of adamant.

DITAN. (*repeating his up-and-down glance, and smiling scornfully*) Ha! you would poke your English fun at a Southern outcast; but beware! (*indicates the position of his stiletto*)

LEONARD. Rubbish! I have a pair of fists, and muscles to match. I'd lick you single-handed—and I love your child.

DITAN. (*after a struggle*) She is yours.

SIR RUBY GLENGORE. (*breaking through the hedge*) Never!

LEONARD. My uncle! Down, rebellious nature.

SIR RUBY. (*to* DITANTIPALPITI) Vagrant, I am a county magistrate; I have seen this damsel, and to see her was to love her. I am a bachelor—she must be mine.

LEONARD. It shall be over my dead body.

SIR RUBY. *What* shall be over your dead body?

LEONARD. No matter. (*to* DITAN.) He is no bachelor; he has a wife.

SIR RUBY. You lie in your throat.

LEONARD. That is anatomically impossible; there isn't room.

DITAN. (*who has been trying to recal the past and failing*) Where have I seen this man?

SIR RUBY. (*to* LINDA) Maiden, I will make you mistress of Whatd'yemaycall'em Hall, Thingumybobshire. Let us fly!

LINDA. Sir Ruby Glengore, this is not the first time you have insulted me; last Tuesday you——

DITAN. *(with a yell)* Sir Ruby Glengore! That name! Those whiskers! *(with concentrated malignity)* Do you remember this face?

SIR RUBY. *(wincing)* N—no.

DITAN. *(taking off his shoe)* Do you remember this *foot?*

SIR RUBY. Yes. It and I have met—before.

DITAN. *(with deeply concealed sarcasm, and action of the leg expressive of kicking)* No, not BEFORE.

SIR RUBY. I bear the mark still. I did not think to meet thee again.

DITAN. Villain, where is my wife? The wife you stole?

SIR RUBY. She is—no more.

DITAN. *(with a sigh of relief)* 'Tis well. But nevertheless, die! *(attempts to stab* SIR RUBY*)*

LINDA. My dear father, that is not hospitable.

LEONARD. *(with epigrammatic hauteur)* A gipsy should never strike anything—but his tent.

ALL THE TRIBE. *(entering)* Hooray!

SIR RUBY. This young man's bearing and manner have interested me much. Ditantipalpiti, I forgive you everything. Leonard, take her, be happy. The entire tribe shall come and live with me at Whatd'yemaycall'm Hall. Perhaps you would not—under the peculiar circumstances—object to my venturing upon a somewhat bold, but at the same time strikingly original, remark—"Bless you, my children!" *(joins the hands of the young people and the curtain comes down with a thousand pounds on their wedding-day)*

THE EVER-SO-LITTLE BEAR;

OR, THE PALE FACES AND THE PUTEMINDECAULDRON INDIANS.

Characters.

PONGOWONGO (*the Great Coal-scuttle, Chief of his Tribe*).
ROWDI. (*Chief of another Tribe*)

PARAMATTA (*the Prairie Flower*)
NATIVE WARRIORS.

SCENE.—*The boundless Prairie, visible as far as the neck stretches.*

Enter a Procession of NATIVE WARRIORS, *with a pipe a-piece,* R. U. E. *They sit in a demi-semi-circle, into which bounds* PONGOWONGO, *the Great Coalscuttle.*

PONGO. Tribe of the Putemindecauldron Indians, sons of the forest and the prairie, partners of Pongowongo's toil, of Pongowongo's feelings, of Pongowongo's fame—— (*sounds of dissent*) Another hiss and I leave off. (*a volley of hisses immediately*) Now I just *shan't* leave off—there.

INDIAN. The Great Coalscuttle has spoken.

PONGO. Which, begging your pardon and granting your grace, the Great Coalscuttle means to go on. (*weeps*)

TWO OF THE WARRIORS. (*who are* NOT *weeping, in a lucid interval*) We shall go. (*they go,* R.)

ALL THE OTHER WARRIORS. (*wiping their eyes*) A good idea—so will *we.* (*they go,* L.)

PONGO. (*solus*) They have left their chief to his mournful reflections—beasts! but no matter; what can you expect from a set of wretches who paint their noses sky-blue, and eat their enemies without vegetables? Never mind, I have made up my mind; I will be civilized.

Here goes. (*is retiring with the firm determination of
becoming civilized immediately, when he is intercepted in
his path and object by another object,* ROWDI *the Ever-so-
Little Bear*)

ROWDI. (*with extraordinary self-possession*) Humph!

PONGO. Let me go by.

ROWDI. (*who is sarcastic*) No, you are base coin, and
cannot pass.

PONGO. (*with obtuse malignity*) I don't see it, and what's
more I *won't* see it.

ROWDI. (*preparing to scalp him*) You shall.

PONGO. (*shutting both eyes*) I won't.

ROWDI. Then die! (*seizes him by the top-knot, and
commences sawing at it with the edge of his tomahawk—
pauses for breath, the tomahawk being out of condition*)

PONGO. Much more of this and you rouse an Indian's
indomitable nature.

ROWDI. These shilling tomahawks of Mappin are
really in ninety-nine cases out of a hundred——

PONGO. (*suddenly*) Ha! I have you now! In ninety-
nine *cases,* eh? They are never *in* cases; they are
always wrapped in paper, and sticking up at the railway
stalls, together with Scotch caps, rugs, cheap literature,
and Callaghan's telescopes. *Now* what do you say?

ROWDI. What do I say? Why that 'twere vain to tell
thee all I feel—and 'twas within a mile of Edinboro' town.

PONGO. Base subterfuge; but it shall not avail you.

E

The palisadoes of the pale faces' dwellings are visible to
the completely undressed eye. I will go to them, and
tell them my private opinion of your character.

Rowdi. Do so; but ere you do so, allow me to repeat
—die! (*is about to kill* Pongowongo *once more, when*
Paramatta *enters, with a rifle across her shoulder, and
transfixes him to the spot--*Rowdi *drops his fell determination, and is for some moments unable to pick it up again*)

Param. Would you lift your hand against an aged
parent?

Rowdi. I would.

Param; Then you are unworthy the name of a British
sailor.

Rowdi. (*trembles*) I—I—am. (*aside*) Confusion! can
she suspect me? What can I do to disarm suspicion? Ha!
I have it. (*to* Paramatta) Beautious daughter of the
pathless prairie——

Pongo. Nothing of the kind; she's the beauteous
daughter of *me*.

Rowdi. To see you leaping the indigenous frog, to
watch you skipping the native novel, to behold you bound
over to keep the peace, and all with the agility of the
wild soft roe of the Highland herring, was to admire you
—to love you. It is true you belong to a nobler and
wealthier tribe than ours, that you revel in riches, all
settled upon yourself, and I am poor indeed; but I will
waive all that. Come to my burning bosom and my
warm wig—I mean my wig-wam. All my fortune I lay
at your feet. (*placing bow and arrows and a postage stamp
on the ground*) All is thine, if you will, as has been before
observed, "be mine." An answer will oblige.

Param. Oh, this struggle between love and a lot of
other things, and to think that a lot of other things are
getting the worst of it. British sailor——

Rowdi. That fatal—them fatal—hem! *those* fatal
words again. What mean you?

Param. (*to her father*) Behold the fiend's war-paint;
look at the devil's tattoo; both sham. He's no more an
Indian than I—hem! than Spurgeon!

Rowdi. Woman, another word, and I forget your sex
and quit the prairies.

PARAM. (*getting more excited as she goes on*) Do you remember Portsmouth Hard? Do you remember Jemima Soft? Do you remember being pressed, and going to sea as flat as possible? Do you remember striking your superior officer by your unintelligent bearing, and being elevated so much that you were actually sent up to the mast-head? Do you remember forming a desperate resolution to drown yourself, and then, with a superhuman effort, actually changing your mind? Do you remember determining to do something and then not doing it? Do you remember dining with the mess and deserting immediately afterwards? Do you?

ROWDI. (*who has now become dogged*) No, I don't.

PARAM. (*at a nonplus*) Don't you?

PONGO. (*with a look of native idiotcy*) I am all abroad. What does it all mean? (*to the audience*) Perhaps our kyind friends can——

ROWDI. No they can't—not one of them.

PARAM. Then there is nothing for it but this. (*takes off her hunting pouch, and puts on a fresh expression*)

ROWDI. Horror! Jemima!

PONGO. My child *not* my child! this is too much for a warrior full of years. (*retires to the back of the stage and snivels*)

PARAM. For years have I worn the unbecoming costume of a wild huntress of the exceedingly uninteresting prairie. For years have I assumed a different expression to my natural one. This, for the first six months, I found wearying, but I gradually became used to it, and I feel

E 2

quite uncomfortable in getting back to my own look.
I swore revenge against you for your deceit; I followed
you in the vessel; I was the man at the wheel, and of
course no one was allowed to speak to me; I tracked you
through the forest; I saw you join the tribe of the
Putemindecauldron Indians—I stole the sleeping daughter
of Pongowongo out of her cradle, and put myself in her
place. I painted myself exactly like her, and the alter-
ation was never discovered, and——

Pongo. (*waking up*) But what became of my dau——

Param. I have never taken my eyes off you since that
day—in the trackless forests, in the boundless prairies,
in the councils of the warriors, in the muffin worries of the
elderly squaws, have I been watching you, and now—(*load-
ing her rifle*) the moment of vengeance has arrived, and——

Pongo. But my daug——

Param. Old man, shut up ! (*takes aim at* Rowdi) Are
you prepared ?

Rowdi. Certainly not. Have pity.

Param. What pity had you for *me* when—but I repeat——

Pongo. I say, you know, about my daugh——

Rowdi. Pongowongo, tell her not to fire, or, at all
events, come and stand before me.

Pongo. See you hanged first.

Rowdi. And this is friendship !

Pongo. My daught——

Param. I wait to hear you say you are prepared.

Rowdi. Hah ! a brilliant idea ! *Will* you continue to
wait until I say I am prepared ?

Param. I will.

Rowdi. Then nothing is wanting but the applause of
our kyind friends who——

Pongo. But about my daughte——

Param. What do you mean ?

Rowdi. Why simply that if you don't intend firing
until I say I am prepared, you will have to wait a con-
siderable time, for *I will never say it*. (*folds his arms, and
is about to put them in an envelope, when* Pongowongo
pertinaciously and interrogatively remarks)

Pongo. Excuse me, but is my daughter——

Param. *That* you shall never know.

PONGO. Then blow cheeks and crack your winds!

(*raves aside*)

ROWDI. Can you forgive me?

PARAM. I can—I do. Take me to your manly bosom, and try to forget the troublous times which have stamped a Reigate Junction of wrinkles upon your manly brow. As for me, I am getting grey, and the prairie has no charms for me. I freely give up the dirt, discomfort, and misery of *al-fresco* existence for the elegant delight and luxuries of civilization and progress.

ROWDI. Unselfish generous darling! Ah, still the same yielding angel; but what is that in the offing? an English ship?

PONGO. (*at back*) There is no offing; this is the prairie, and the sea's miles away.

PARAM. Poor old man; his mind still wanders. Come, let us for England, ho!

ROWDI. But first——

PARAM. What?

PONGO. (*cutting in*) Why our kyind friends——

PARAM. Oh, ah; may they never forget the lesson of to-night, but may it sink into the innermost recesses of their waistcoats, and console them in the chilling hours of coming winter, for though a burnt child fears the fire, the heart that can feel for another can also appreciate the charms of our uncultivated nature, and the rude, though simple-minded manners of the copper-coloured children of the Prairies of our Western Wilds.

Highland Reel and Curtain.

ALLURIO AND ADELINA;

OR,

THE VILLAGE INN AND THE COUNT OUT.

A MODEL ENGLISH OPERA.

Characters.

ALLURIO (*a Swiss Lover*)
COUNT CRACKALOBSTERCLAWSKI (*a Wanderer*).
ADELINA (*the Village Beauty*).

SCENE.—*A Tyrolean Village, with the highly respectable hostel, the " Flea and Earthquake," to the right about face of the stage. A signboard is swinging in the wind, and creaks harmoniously with the chorus. The mountains of the Tyrol are seen at the back, and hardy Mountaineers are climbing about, with no particular object, except an occasional English Traveller—upon the extremity of the peak of the tallest an adventurous Briton is seen reading a red " Murray," and smoking a cigar with the phlegmatic indifference of his insular nature—the chamois is " bounding wild" in several places, and two avalanches are having a race down one mountain, while a procession of Proprietors of " buy-a-brooms," " hurdy-gurdies," and white mice is seen crossing another—all is bright, clean, and pleasant, and a general air of " Tra la la" pervades the landscape.*

Enter on the right six MALE PEASANTS, *preternaturally clean, with turn-down collars, worked braces, and everything agreeable.*

Chorus.—MALE PEASANTS.

Oh, rapture, joy and bliss !
Oh, what a day is this ;
The sun is shining,
Not declining,
Oh, rapture, joy, and bliss !

SIX FEMALE PEASANTS *entering left side.*

> Oh, bliss, oh, rapture, joy!
> Oh, bliss without alloy;
> To-day's the day,
> The tenth of May,
> Oh, bliss, oh, rapture, joy!

ALL.
> Joy, joy, joy,
> Bliss, bliss, bliss,
> Rapture, rapture, rapture,
> Without
> Al——
> Loy!

1ST PEASANT. Yes, 'tis Adelina's wedding morning. She is the pride of the village.

ALL. She *is.*

2ND PEASANT. She is an orphan!

ALL. Just so.

1ST PEASANT. But see, she comes!

ALL. She do!

Light music—Enter ADELINA.

M. PEASANTS. Hoo——

F. PEASANTS. Ray!

M. PEASANTS. Bray——

F. PEASANTS. Vo!

ADELINA. Loved ones, it breaks my heart to think I'm so soon to leave you.

1ST PEASANT. The thought has stamped wrinkles on

our manly brows and thinned the flowing locks of several;
but we are men, and we will bear it. Where do you think
of settling?

ADEL. (*shrinking*) Do—do not ask me.

1ST PEASANT. (*aside*) There is something on her mind.
(*aloud*) Has Allurio deceived thee?

ALL. (*drawing their knives*) Ha!

ADEL. No, no. But perhaps a ditty of our native clime
would not be, under the circumstances, inappropriate. Here
goes.

Tyrolean Ballad.

The avalanche is falling
    Down the rocky mountain's side,
And the chamois is a calling
    To his beauteous bounding bride,
And the pine tree o'er the chasms
    But a trifling footing lends,
And the traveller has the spasms—
    When the bridge so fragile bends.

(*andantino*) And the traveller has the spasms,

M. PEASANTS. (*forte*) The spasms——

ADEL.   Yes, the trav'ller has the spasms,

F. PEASANTS. (*pianissimo*) The spasms——

ADEL.   When the bridge so fragile bends.
          But—(*slight pause*)

(*with rapturous nationality*) Tra, la la, tral la la,
            Tra la la la lah,
            Tra la la, tral, la la,
            Tra la la la lah!

(*Chorus, "Tra la la" as long as the Audience
will permit, and the* PEASANTS *go off the stage
up various mountain paths, leaving* ADELINA *alone*)

ADEL. I am alone, and the mountain air is somewhat
bleak, but wrapped in my Magenta bodice and conscious
innocence, I can afford to brave the fury of the elements.
Where is Allurio? It is our wedding morning, and he is
not here; something must have happened to him. Some·
thing always *is* happening in these unfettered wilds of
bounteous nature. (*sits,* R.)

Enter ALLURIO, R., *a young man with a high voice and low*
principles.

ALLURIO. Ha! I did not think these hands would ever
become stained with crime. But what could I do? He is
rich, and I am poor. The wedding ring was fourteen
shillings, and I had them not. We were crossing a
mountain gorge together—no one was by—a short struggle,
and it was all over; that's to say *he* was all over. 'Tis
strange, but ever since I have committed the crime I have
felt most uncomfortable—p'raps it's conscience; if so, it
must be smothered. Ah! how true it is—(*looking very hard
at the leader of the orchestra, who is not paying proper
attention*) *I say how true it is* that it is impossible to drown
the screams of a guilty and blood-stained breast.

Song.—" *The Blood-stained Breast."*
(WRITTEN FOR THE MUSIC PUBLISHERS.)

The blood-stained breast will never rest,
    And conscience *won't* be dumb;
The wicked heart at each fresh start
    Goes tum te tum te tum.

        (*Tyrolean echo of the last line*)

Oh bliss for ever past is now,
    'Twere vain to tell thee all
I feel—I feel—I feel—I vow—
    I feel (*slight pause*) uncommon small.

They say that murder has a knack
    Of always coming out.
Oh, Maid of Athens, give me back—
    Pooh! what am I about?

Far, far upon the sea, as sings
    H. Russell, I'll seek rest;
Oh, gracious me, what anguish wrings
    The bursting, blood-stained breast.

(*at the conclusion of the song* ALLURIO *retires to the
    back gloomily and* ADELINA *comes down to the
    footlights*)

ADEL. There is something on his mind. I will see if a ditty of his native clime will soothe his pallid but agitated feelings. (*goes up to* ALLURIO *playfully, and sings in a coquettish manner*)

Oh, Tra la la,
Tra la la,
Tra——

ALLUR. There, leave off tra la la-ing. It's a nuisance.

ADEL. Oh, Allurio, this is unkind. There is something troubling you; confide in me—if it's acidity, say so.

ALLUR. Oh, Adelina, we were to have been married to-day, but—but it must be broken off.

ADEL. (*agonizedly*) *What* must be broken off?

ALLUR. The match. It is the tenth of May !

ADEL. Match! May! (*aside*) His mind is wandering. Dear one, do you allude to Bryant and May's matches, which "ignite only on the box ?"

ALLUR. Woman, temptress, *nothing* ignites on the box—(*after a reflective pause*) except à 'bus driver's cigar. Ha, ha !

ADEL. I see ; forgetful of our early vows, regardless of the one true simple heart that loves you, reckless of the tender feelings of the mountain maiden, you—you've been drinking rum and water before breakfast.

ALLUR. 'Tis false !

ADEL. The air is poisoned, Allurio, with the odour of your unnaturally early nip.

ALLUR. I see you love an-odour. If he exists in this hamlet——

ADEL. Talk not of Hamlet. You are more an " on tick rum'un than a Dane." Hem, Shakespeare.

ALLUR. Don't know the gentleman; but if he has trifled with your affections—or Bryant, or May—in sooth you seem to have a number of friends *I* have never heard of before—I say if *any* of them have trifled—but no matter ; ha, ha! no matter—I can bear it. (*seizes a pewter pot from the table by the inn door and tears it to atoms*)

ADEL. Cowardly Allurio ; but I will be even with you ; I also possess the sensibility of an insulted female. (*pulls out a photograph of* ALLURIO) There ! (*treads upon it*)

ALLUR. Ha, how true are the words of the inspired Falconer and Chatterton (authors of the "Shipwreck" and "Perished in his Pride") that "Nature's above Art."

ADEL. Hold your tongue!

ALLUR. Hold yours! False one. I love thee still.　In fact you can't be *too* still.

ADEL. Monster!

ALLUR. You're another.　I will never see thee more—farewell for ever!

ADEL. Ay, for ever!

Duet.

ALLUR. I'll seek in foreign climes a home,
　　　　　I cannot linger here.

ADEL. Go brave the boist'rous billows foam,
　　　　　I will not shed a tear.

ALLUR. Oh, heartless maid.
ADEL. 　　Oh, cruel man.
ALLUR. Betrayed, betrayed.
ADEL. Oh, how you can!

ALLUR. } *(ensemble)* { I'll seek, etc.
ADEL. 　}　　　　　　　{ Go seek, etc.

　　(ALLURIO *rushes off,* L., *and* ADELINA *falls on the stage
　　　regardless of her worsted lover and her sarcenet
　　　bow. The music changes, and the* COUNT CRACKA-
　　　LOBSTERCLAWSKI *comes on,* R. U. E.—*he is tall,
　　　melancholy, pallid, and mysterious*)

Recitative.

COUNT. Yes, 'tis the village!
ORCHESTRA. Tum te tum.
COUNT. There is the pump!
ORCHESTRA. Te tum te toddy.
COUNT. And there the old church spire.
ORCHESTRA. Te tum, te tum, te tiddidol.
COUNT. Ah me, what feelings;
ORCHESTRA. Te tum te teedum.
COUNT. And particularly indescribable sensations;
FLUTE. Toodle-oodle-oodle (*ad lib.*)
COUNT. Get over me.
ORCHESTRA. (*fortissimo*) Tiddle-iddle-iddle-um TUM!

Ballad.

COUNT.   'Twas here I met the only maiden
           I ever did adore;
           Though quite grown up, she was arrayed in
           A pin—a pinafore.

           We met, we loved, we parted,
           She made her will and died,
           She left me broken-hearted,
           And nothing else beside.

The sight of these well-known spots recalls to my recollection the bitter memories of the past. Every point
in the picture produces a pang. How can I view yon
crumbling spire without reflecting on the decayed beauty
of my lost one, and does not that tall pump remind me of
my own heartless self? Existence is a burden; I will put
an end to it. I have seen "Manfred," but it has failed to
chase the gloomy cloud from my brow. Yon mountain
top reminds me of the moments and marbles of youthful
innocence. I will ascend it, and when I have reached its
snow-clad summit, I will revenge myself upon my fellow-
men by turning round and coming down again.

        (*he is about to put this fearful resolve into execution
        when he sees the prostrate form of* ADELINA)

Recitative.

What's that? A girl! and of the female sex!
ADEL. (*sitting up*) Where am I?
COUNT. Hee-ar!
ADEL. Say, who are you?
COUNT. I am—oh, 'evans!
ADEL. Evans? don't know him.
COUNT. (*aside*) That nose! 'Tis mine!
ADEL. (*retreating*) Nay, sir, 'tis mine.

Duet.

COUNT. What's this feeling o'er me stealing,
      Like a dream of bygone bliss?
      Instantly to me revealing
      Be your name and station, miss.

ADEL. Vain would be attempts to smother
      My lone situation sad;
      I've no father nor no mother,
      No, nor what's more, never had.

COUNT. Adelina, concealment on my part would be ridiculous; stay—tell me—have you any property?
ADEL. Yes, a snug little fortune.
COUNT. Then I am your lost long father—at least, long lost father. Come to Count Crackalobsterclawski's waistcoat; it is scared and desolate, but in the fashion. (ADELINA *rushes into his arms*)

Enter Allurio, *l. u. e.*, *who only perceives the mutual embrace, and not the features of the* Count.

Allur. What do I see? Oh, faithless one!

Adel. I've found him!

Allur. (*tucking up his sleeves*) You've *found* him; but I shall *hide* him. Come on! (*the* Count *turns to* Allurio. *who, on beholding his face, sinks, shakes, and turns livid*)

Allur. Alive! While you were crossing the mountains with me you fell down in a crack in a rock.

Count. (*with an aristocratic skip*) Yes, but I got *up* in a crack.

Allur. Impossible!

Count. Not so, for remember I am a *climbing Pole*. (Allurio *and* Adelina *burst into tears and fall at* Count's *feet*)

Count. I see everything at a glance. Take her! be happy; I will come and live with you. The Village Inn is to let—you must take it. Don't think I shall desert you; no; my children, I will never, never leave you. Here comes the villagers; it is time you were married; a jorum of something (by-the-way, I have no small change about me), just to drink the health of my new-found children, and then hey for the parson and perpetual happiness.

The Chorus *having re-entered, cleaner (if possible) than ever.*

Finale.

ALL.   Oh, rapture, joy and bliss!
           Oh, what a day is this;

The sun is shining,
Not declining,
Oh, rapture, joy, and bliss.

Oh, bliss, oh, rapture, joy!
Oh, bliss without alloy;
To-day's the day,
The tenth of May,
Oh, bliss, oh, rapture, joy.

(ADELINA *comes forward, and indulges in what
appears to be a satirical vocal dissection of the
melody, lasting over twenty minutes, and re-
sembling an ineffectual attempt to sing " Il Bacio,"
" Rode's Air," with variations, the " Puritani
Polacca," and the " Scales," all at the same time.
The House and Curtain come down simultaneously*)

GOLD AND GUILT;

OR,

THE TRUE RING OF THE GENUINE METAL.

A MORE THAN ORDINARILY STANDARD COMEDY.

In Five Acts (Founded on the best Muddles).

Characters.

LORD LUSHBOROUGH.
PERCY PENTONVILLE.
HON. TOM TIPTOP (*his Friend*).
FARMER MERRYPEBBLES.
SLIME (*Lord Lushborough's Steward*).
MAUD MERRYPEBBLES.

ACT I.

SCENE.—*Library at Lushborough Hall. Furnished by Messrs. Gillow, Jackson and Graham, Brown, Jones, Robinson, and Smith.*

Enter SLIME, L.—*he looks round (being exceedingly stout), and rubs his hands together with a repulsive grin—after chuckling for some moments (a great artistic resource, as it enables the audience to settle down quietly) he comes down to the footlights and commences.*

SLIME. Ha! ha! This is the fourth of August. Oysters come in on this eventful day—but no matter. He who thinks he is my master—but never mind. And I—*I*, who am accounted his willing tool, his slave, his—but no more of this. He is here.

Enter LORD LUSHBOROUGH, R.

SLIME. Good morning, my lord.
LORD L. (*starting—aside*) Hah! what means that suspicious observation? I fear me that old man has more in him than meets the eye.

SLIME. I hope your lordship is well.

LORD L. (*starting more violently even than before*) Again, a significant and mysterious sentence which baffles me. Tush, this is weakness. (*aloud*) Slime, you have ever been the recipient of my inmost thoughts, the sharer of my every private feeling, the counsellor of my youthful days, the valued friend of my more advanced years.

SLIME. I have, my lord.

LORD L. Then get out.

Exit SLIME, *with a peculiar expression of countenance*, R.

LORD L. That old man is virtuous and a bore. Everything virtuous, I abominate, save Maud! She comes.

Enter MAUD, *an under-housemaid in Lord Lushborough's establishment*, L., *she carries a dust pan and brush, and has on a pair of housemaid's gloves.*

MAUD. My lord!

LORD L. My Maud!

MAUD. Pardon me, my lord, I am *not* your Maud. I am 'umble, and born of poor but honest parents, and, though of lowly birth, the simple farmer's daughter can afford to despise, aye, my lord, to despise (*looking him up and down, and then down and up*) my noble Lord-a-Lushborough. Let me pass; I came to light your lordship's library fire.

LORD L. Maud—more beautiful in the housemaid's glove of conscious innocence, than in the six and a quarter Houbigant of gilded vice; oh——

MAUD. Houbigant! *You* be gone!

LORD L. Never! Come, dear Maud, let us fly far away from this hated country—far away to the sunny South, where the golden cockroach dances in the sunlight, and the wine is ruby bright. Come, dwell with me and be my love; come unto these yellow sands; come where the aspens quiver, come.

FARMER MERRYPEBBLES. (*entering suddenly*, L.) Come, I say, you're a " coming" it pretty strong, my lord, I think.

MAUD. Father! (*rushes into her parent's arms*)

FARMER M. Ay, girl, twine thine arms round feyther's neck, nestle up agin feyther's weskit; it's a numble one may be, but it covers a heart that never stooped its knee

F

to the sway of an oppressor, or took off its hat to a coward and a willin!

Lord L. Leave my house, fellow, and take with you your minikin daughter. Stay, take off your housemaid's gloves, young woman, they are my property.

Farmer M. Ay, lass, off with 'em. (*throws them at Lord Lushborough's feet*) You may raise my rent (it's as much as I can do mysen), you may turn us barefoot into the stony roads, you may break my ould heart; but you shall never rob me of the one ray of sunshine that's gladdened my home, and cleaned her poor father's boots from a infant, not if you was twenty Lords of the Manor, as sure as my name's Mat Merrypebbles!

Lord L. Away! or I will order my lackeys to thrust ye from my portals! Away! (*sinks into a chair*—Maud *and her* Father *move towards the door*)

Slime. (*who has noiselessly entered,* R., *aside*) Ha! Ha! He is in the toils. He is in the toils.

(*the drop descends slowly*)

ACT II.

Scene.—*Magnificently furnished Apartment in the Albany —everything suggestive of bachelor luxury—elegant sofas, splendid pictures, and handsomely bound books—the scene is flavoured with Latakia tobacco (from Hudson's).*

PERCY PENTONVILLE, *in a dressing gown (by Poole) and slippers (from Hoby's), is reclining on a couch talking to the* HONOURABLE TOM TIPTOP, *who is twiddling a*

cane *(from the eminent establishment of Mr. Martin, Burlington-arcade), and applying a toothpick (maker's name mislaid, to his white teeth (periodically looked to by Mr. Robinson), and running his hand through his hair (parted by Truefitt)*

HON. TOM TIPTOP. Foregad, Percy, you must marry! It's a duty you owe to society; you must settle down; you can't go on breaking girls' hearts in this way ever so many times a season. Look at Georgina Jollysquint; hasn't she taken to working High Church parson's mediæval braces and middle-age slippers in despair. Then there's the Dowager Lady Duckinthunder, young, rich, lovely, married only a week, husband broke his neck hunting—she's ready for you with her half-a-million any moment. As for Celestina Sopinpan, Araminta Spoonbill, and all three of the Oozlybird girls, they're fretting themselves into skeletons for you. Egad, sir, you must marry, and stop this wholesale heartbreaking.

PERCY. A truce to this badinage, Tom. I have seen none that I should care to marry. For mark me, I will never wed until I find one worthy of me, never.

HON. T. *(aside)* Noble, generous-hearted fellow.

PERCY. Besides, you know my peculiar position. A foundling, supported by voluntary contributions. Kept like a prince by some unknown friend, who sends me up

F 2

a thousand pounds every quarter, and never lets me
know who he is or who I am. Oh, Tom, Tom, who—
who am I?

HON. T. The best fellow in the three kingdoms; the
crackest shot, the boldest rider, the cleverest whip, the
fastest waltzer, the modern Crichton, the eighth wonder of
the world.

PERCY. I am afraid you flatter me.

HON. T. Not a bit.

PERCY. Well, perhaps not. (*a knock*) Come in.

Enter FARMER MERRYPEBBLES, L. (*very much aged since the
last Act, having lost most of his hair, and his calves, and
much of his manliness ; his waistcoat hangs loose, and his
back is very much bowed*) — MAUD *accompanies him—
she has on a little straw hat with cherry-coloured ribbons,
and looks sorrow stricken, but natty.*

FARMER M. (*in weak tones*) Which is Mr. Percy
Pentonville ?

PERCY. I am he.

MAUD. Then, sir, if you please, as we were coming to
London, we were desired to give you this. (*hands him a
letter*)

PERCY. (*aside*) What a lovely girl. How different
from the artificial beauties of the glittering salons of the
aristocracy. (*opens the letter*) Hah, my quarter's allowance!
Now I shall know who is my unknown benefactor. (*to
MAUD*) Tell me, fair maiden, who gave you this ?

MAUD. I was told not to say, sir, and though 'umble, I never disgraced my honest name by telling a crammer.

PERCY. (*aside*) How elegantly she expresses herself. (*to* MAUD) Pardon me, but your refined speech but ill accords with your humble gyarb. You interest me much.

MAUD. (*aside*) What is this strange sensation? Can it be love? Oh, I feel as I have never felt before. When I gaze upon the lordly whiskers of this noble youth, how common and low appears the vulgar old bald head of my plebeian pa. (*turning to her father sharply*) Come on; this is no place for us.

PERCY. Your name, fair damsel?

MAUD. Maud.

HON. T. And a deuced pretty name too, my girl.

PERCY. (*to* TOM) Sir, scoundrel! you have insulted a lady, and beneath my roof. This afternoon a friend of mine shall call upon ye.

MAUD. Gentlemen! gentlemen!

FARMER M. Let my grey hairs have some influence——

HON. T. Pah, fight with *you*—with a nameless *pauper*!

PERCY. Let me get at him! (*is about to rush upon him, when* SLIME *enters suddenly,* L., *and arrests the blow—picture*)

SLIME. What would ye do? Rash boy, reserve your wrath for others.

PERCY. Nameless! Nameless! (*sinks into a chair in an agony of conscious insignificance;* MAUD *falls into her Father's arms; the* HONOURABLE TOM TIPTOP *curls his aristocratic upper lip, and* SLIME *rubs his hands and grins sardonically*)

SLIME. (*aside*) Ha! ha! ha! It works bravely; it works bravely. Ha! ha! ha! (*drop descends*)

ACT III.

SCENE.—*A Room in Lushborough Hall.*

Enter SLIME.

SLIME. (*chuckling*) Ha! ha!—— (*drop descends—some hours are supposed to elapse before Act IV.*)

ACT IV.

SCENE.—*An Apartment in Lushborough Hall.*

SLIME. (*concluding the chuckle commenced in Act III.*) HAH ! (*drop descends quickly*)

ACT V.

SCENE.—*Drawing Room at Lushborough Hall.*

LORD LUSHBOROUGH *alone.*

LORD L. What is this strange feeling which depresses me? It is either the gnawing of a guilty conscience, or the uncommingling perversity of the marmalade and game pie I was so absent as to devour simultaneously at my breakfast. Who would think that the wakeful miseries of one feverish night would have stamped so many wrinkles on my brow and grizzled the ebon locks but yesterday as black as— (*a loud peal of thunder heard*) —thunder. Pshaw! Tush! Pish! Bosh! Rubbish! I will shake off this melancholy, and be lively. (*attempts a double shuffle, and shrieks with a wild laugh*) With a *Heup*-de-dooden-*Doo !* (*relapses into gloom*) It is in vain; melancholy has marked me for her own.

Enter PERCY PENTONVILLE *in a cloak,* L.

PERCY. I fear me I intrude.

LORD L. Sirrah! This is *my* house.

SLIME *enters suddenly with* MAUD, FARMER MERRYPEBBLES, *and* HON. TOM TIPTOP, L.

SLIME. A lie! a base and cowardly lie! Viper! Toad! Thief!

LORD L. This language, even in an old and faithful servant, smacks somewhat of the personal. (*aside*) My olfactory powers begin to assure me of the presence of a burrowing and unpleasant quadruped.

SLIME. This *your* house! It's *mine*.

ALL THE OTHERS. Mine! (*correcting themselves*) Yours !

SLIME. Behold the rightful heir! (*points to* PERCY)

You, my lord. are an impostor—a puppet I placed in power; I dallied with the strings so long as it suited my purpose. The late lord left his will to *his* son, who was stolen when young. *I* stole him—no matter why—it was my humour. Here is the will; you were the next of kin—but not now. Ha! ha! ha! not now, not now. (*retires to back and continues chuckling until fall of curtain*)

LORD L. And this is the end of crime. (*gaily*) Nampot! Away to the gambling table and the turf! and veve la baggytell!

PERCY. Will you accept my hand *now*, Maude?

MAUD. Oh, yes!

PERCY. Unselfish angel, she refused me when unknown; but, now that I have a title and estates, she is——

MAUD. Thine, dear Percy, thine.

FARMER M. (*who has become drivelling during the third and fourth acts*) Yes, lass, full Percy is better nor empty Percy.

HON. T. Egad, my old buck, you're in the right of it, so hey for the parson and——

MAUD. Firstly, though, we must obtain the consent of those merry faces we see around us, who, let us trust, will kindly continue to smile upon our tale of "GOLD AND GUILT; OR——

PERCY. (*with conjuror-like rapidity producing a wedding-ring from his waistcoat pocket*) "THE TRUE RING OF THE GENUINE METAL." (SLIME *still chuckling*)

Curtain.

FULL PRIVATE PERKINS;

OR,

"HE WIPED AWAY A TEAR."

A MILITARY DRAMA.

Characters.

MAJOR-GENERAL BUNGALOW BROWN, *of Her Majesty's Twenty-second Rebuffs.*
FULL PRIVATE PERKINS, *an Orphan.*
DAME MAYDEW.
ROSE MAYDEW.
OFFICERS *and* GENTLEMEN.

ACT I.

SCENE.—*A Cottage in the Country. The Village of Umbleworth seen in the distance—the palings in front of the cottage are painted a village green, and contentment is seen distinctly hovering over the building as the curtain rises—real smoke rises from the chimney, and life-like rurality is given to the scene by a mingled odour of bacon and clematis (registered) being wafted through the house.*

DAME MAYDEW *enters from cottage with* ROSE.

DAME. No, Rose; I fear he will never come back. A Private Perkins was shot in the mutiny.

ROSE. Pardon me, dear mother, he was shot in the elbow.

DAME. Well, perhaps you are right. I am getting old and deaf, and never larnt to spell. Ah, there was no such thing as larning in my young days; young girls used to spin their flax, and make their puddings, and go to market, and see to the poultry, and—— (*military march heard*)

ROSE. Hah, what mean those inspiring sounds? It's the soldiers! (*blushes*)

DAME. Beware of 'em, my child. Don't bring dis-

honour on your parent's name. Remember your father,
who never went to bed sober for thirty years, and died in
a fit, after beating me black and blue, and don't disgrace
his honoured memory. Them soldiers is all bad—except
my 'Arry, my poor lost 'Arry. (*weeps*)

Rose. The music has died away in the distance..

Dame. Just like 'Arry, *he* died away in the distance,
with no one to smooth his clammy brow—no one to
moisten his parched lips, and no one to learn where he'd
put all his "loot," and how the Delhi prize money was
to be got at.

Enter a Mysterious Stranger, *more than ordinarily
muffled up,* L.

Stranger. Can any one tell me if Full Private Perkins
lives here?

Rose. He *did* live here, sir, long, oh, very long——

Stranger. Six feet two, or thereabouts.

Rose. Yes, sir, in his stockings.

Stranger. But *out* of them?

Rose. I never saw him *out* of them, sir. (*retires behind*
Dame)

Stranger. (*aside*) The same beauteous love of truth
as ever. (*aloud*) And you, old lady, can you——

Dame. Old lady, forsooth! let me tell you, if my
adopted son, 'Arry Perkins, which he is full private in Her
Majesty's Twenty-second Rebuffs, was alive he would
not permit such insolent remarks. Proceed, sir, on your
way; you mean him no good, or you would not heap con-
tumely on the whitened hair of a broken-hearted parent.

Stranger. (*aside*) I can bear this suspense, and this
heavy cloak no longer. (*loudly, discovering himself*)
Mother! (Dame Maydew *and* Rose *shriek, then exclaiming*
"'Arry," *rush wildly into the arms of the quondam
stranger*)

Private P. And you, Rose, how you have grown;
you are quite a woman. But you have not forgotten
your early playmate?

Rose. Forgotten you? Oh, 'Arry, could you deem
me false?

Private P. No, dear one. I look into those blue eyes

and see my own image reflected in all its soldier-like
truthfulness: but what else is this I see reflected?
Major-General Bungalow Brown. Ha, he comes across
the fields—he gets over the stile—he is here. (*turns and
salutes* MAJOR-GENERAL BUNGALOW BROWN, *who has
entered*, L.)

GENERAL. Ha, ha! Snug quarters, Perkins: day-vilish
snug quarters. (*shakes himself, coughs with military huskiness,
and pulls himself together after the manner of stage
martinets*)

PRIVATE P. General, this visit is indeed a honour.
Let me present you to my mother—leastways——

GENERAL. Mrs. Leastways, I am proud to know you.
Your son is a brave young man; the way in which he
brought up the rear in the battle of Pepperypotteryhydery-
bang, and the manner in which he led the forlorn hope
and boldly lighted the military train that blew up the
lemonade power mills, together with the manner in which
he flung himself before his General and insisted upon
receiving two bullets intended for me in his own manly
bosom—all this, I say, convinced me that he only wanted
an opportunity to do something really plucky. That
opportunity has not yet presented itself, but it will, and
I feel certain that when the occasion arises Full Private
Perkins will not disgrace the honourable uniform he bears.

PRIVATE P. These words are too much—too much.
(*retires to back with* DAME MAYDEW, *and they mingle
their tears*)

GENERAL. And so you are the pretty Rose we have so
often heard of, eh?

Rose. I suppose so, sir. I—a—that is——

General. (*aside*) Her confusion is delicious. Would it be considered impertinent if an old soldier were to salute those cherry lips?

Rose. It would.

General. Nay, I will not be denied.

Rose. Beware, sir. My station is lowly, but virtue has gilded our humble roof.

General. Bother your humble roof! Is an old weather-beaten General, who has risen from the ranks, and been battered about in all parts of the world and most parts of his body, to give away before the frown of a bit of a girl! No! Dash my epaulets, I'll have a kiss. (*struggle*)

Private P. (*coming down*) Hah! What do I see? My Rose in the military embraces of a Major-General! Away subordination and respect! Die! (*knocks down the* General)

General. Full Private Perkins. 'Tention! (Private Perkins *stands stiff as a poker, with his hands slapped down to his thighs in the regulation attitude*) You have struck your ruperior sofficer—that is to say, offerior supicer—hem! this sudden blow has somewhat confused me. You have hit your Major-General in the eye. It hurts your Major-General, and your Major-General orders you under arrest. Go to your quarters and deliver yourself up to the guard. Quick mar-r-r-r-oooh!

(*Music*—Private Perkins *refuses to run away, as* Dame Maydew *and* Rose *strongly advise him in*

dumb show, but takes himself into custody, hand-
cuffs himself, forms himself into a square, and
*marches off—*Rose *faints in Dame Maydew's arms,*
and the Major-General *looks after* Perkins, *and*
*then goes off to look after his eye—*Perkins *is seen*
to turn upon his heel to " take a last fond look," and
upon this touching reminiscence of the familiar song
the Curtain slowly descends)

ACT II.

Scene.—*A Court Martial.*

Officers *seated uncomfortably, and trying very hard to*
*look like Judges, but failing dismally—*General Louis
Napoleon Abe Skidama Lincoln *is President.*

Opening Chorus.

There's nothing so prime as a pleasant Court-Martial,
With pris'ner so humble and judges impartial;
Our su-preme authority no one can doubt,
So Full Private Perkins had better look out.

Cornet Potts. (*rising*) Gentlemen, I rise to propose—
Brother Officers. Order! Order! Order!
President. I think it scarcely——
Mr. F. Toole. (*specially retained*) Pray si-lence for
the chair!
Presid. Bring in the prisoner.
Mr. Harker. (*specially retained on the other side*) Pray
silence for the prisoner.

    (*Vault's Music—the* Prisoner *is brought in from his*

dungeon, R.—MAJOR-GENERAL BUNGALOW BROWN
*is accommodated with a seat, and a glass of brandy
and water on the bench*)

PRESID. Full Private Perkins, you are charged with
hitting your superior officer in the eye.

GENERAL. *This* one. (*hands it round for the inspection
of the Court, as it is a glass one*)

CORNET P. (*aside*) Glasses round.

MR. HARKER. Si-lence!

MR. F. TOOLE. (*unprofessionally*) Hold *your* row.

PRIVATE P. I *did* hit my superior officer, if he *is* my
superior. The aristocracy of birth is—— (*aristocratic
groans from* LIEUTENANT LANKY, *whose grandfather commenced life as a locksmith*)

PRESID. Do you plead guilty or not guilty?

PRIVATE P. Oh, guilty, by all means.

PRESID. Then the sentence of the Court is—— (DAME
MAYDEW *rushes in with* ROSE, L.)

DAME. Where is he, my son? (*in the confusion of the
moment embraces the* PRESIDENT—*horror on the part of*
LIEUTENANT LANKY, *at the plebeian birth of his superior*)

PRESID. This intrusion is ill-timed. The sentence of
the Court is——

ROSE. It isn't.

PRESID. The sight of the prisoner's relations unmans
me. So it does all of us. Don't it, brother officers?

ALL *but Cornet Potts.* It does.

CORNET P. It don't unman *me*. We all know what
women are made of.

ROSE. (*in a state of sudden imbecility*)
Sugar and spice,
And all things nice,
And *that's* what young women are made of.

DAME. See, gentlemen, she raves.

PRIVATE P. I am prepared to meet my fate; go it, Court.

PRESID. The sentence of the Court is ——.

GENERAL. (*having finished his glass*) Stay, I relent——

EVERYBODY. Ha!

GENERAL. There is something about him that reminds
me of my long-lost son.

EVERYBODY. Ha!

GENERAL. Prisoner at the bar, have you got the mark of a waggon and four horses in the small of your back?

PRIVATE P. (*looking*) I have.

GENERAL. Then come to my arms. (*the* GENERAL *embraces* PRIVATE PERKINS, DAME MAYDEW *embraces the* PRESIDENT, CORNET POTTS *embraces* LIEUTENANT LANKY, *and* MR. F. TOOLE *embraces* MR. HARKER) You horrid old woman, why didn't you restore my son to me before?

DAME. I was a going to do it jest as the soldiers was a aiming at him.

PRIVATE P. Mother, that was indiscreet.

GENERAL. To prevent his being shot I withdraw the charge; my dear boy only struck me—by his manly conduct. Take her, you young dog, and if you, dear madam, will accept——

DAME. (*curtseying*) Oh! anythink, sir, as you please to give.

GENERAL. Then, there's my hand, and egad, we'll have a double wedding.

MR. F. TOOLE. Three cheers for Major-General Bungalow Brown, and please to take the time from *me!*

MR. HARKER. (*with mild ferocity*) Excuse me, from ME, if you please.

ROSE. A truce to these dissensions, and if our kyind friends will only smile upon our efforts there will be nothing wanting to complete the happiness of——

PRIVATE P. " FULL PRIVATE PERKINS ; OR,——

GENERAL. (*regardless of the context or the consequences*) "HE WIPED AWAY A TEAR."

Curtain.

THE
WHITE ROSE OF THE PLANTATION;

OR,

LUBLY ROSA, SAMBO DON'T COME.

A NEGRO DRAMA.

Characters.

Growls (an *Overseer*).
Cincinnatus (*a polished Black*).
Pete (*an old Nigger*).
Rosa (*called " The White Rose of the Plantation."*)

Scene.—*A Cotton Field, in which several* Negroes *are picking the plant.* Overseers *with whips are looking on; and in the back distance is distinctly observable, lending an enchantment to the view without interest. Two Oc-*toroons *and one* Maccaroon *are down in the front, and one old* Negro *with a hump is up in the back.*

Opening Chorus.

Down in Tennessee—
Uly, oley, EE—
Massa, misses, me,
And Pickaninnee
Went out for a spree
And put out my knee,
Uly, oley, EE.

Rosa. (*coming down*) See the sun is sinking
Down behind a cloud,
And the moon like winking,
Not by no means proud
Is a gently rising
Like a thingumbob.
Oh! how appetizing
Is the sweet corn cob.

Dance around the kettle,
　In the dough nut pop,
Let the dripping settle—
　Settle at the top.

ALL THE SLAVES. Down in Tennessee—
　Uly, oley, EE—
Flip up in de skid a majink,
With a riddle cum dinky dee,

(*Ecstatic Dance on the part of the* NEGROES—*after the dance most of the* SLAVES *retire to their quarters, except the married ones, who go to their better halves. The stage is untenanted save by* ROSA, *who is alone and unhappy*)

ROSA. I am alone. The merry sons of toil have retired to their happy homes, having picked the requisite time, namely, thirty-two hours out of the twenty-four, while I—I—but let me drown my miseries in a wild ditty of my youthful days.

Song.

'Twas in the dismal swamp,
　Where my father had the cramp,
And my mother had a chronic rheumatiz-tiz-tiz;
　And where my brothers six,
　Had sciatica like bricks,
For its p'r'aps the dampest neighbourhood as is-is-is.

It was one afternoon,
I think but very soon,
After *I'd* recovered from the ague, or, or, or,
Neuralgia, can't say which,
That young Lorrimor so rich,
A coming down the road just by I sor, sor, sor.

Says he, " Your name, I pray ?"
Says I, " Sir, Rosa May ;"
Says he, " I'll marry you upon the spot, spot, spot ;
But as there was no church,
He left me in the lurch,
And marry me of course why he could not, not, not.

Though I'd a chronic cold,
I very soon was sold,
Oh, miles away from Lorrimor, but he, he, he,
Some day I'm sure will come,
And Rosa will ran-som
Down here in melancholy Tennessee-see-see.

(Rosa *retires as* Growls, *the overseer, enters,* R.)

Growls. There she is a settin' by herself, like the sun. When I look upon that girl all my past life rushes afore me like a penny-rammer. Oh, 'orror ! likewise remorse ! also despair ! (*weeps*)

Rosa. Ha ! Growls, and weeping too.

Growls. Oh, Rosa, once I was as innocent as you—innocenter I may say; but now ! Oh Rosa, I have done things as would make your hair curdle and your blood stand on end. I was scarcely four when I killed my father, in a mortal struggle, and he was soon followed by my mother, who crossed my path and shared his fate. I had a brother—a little chubby boy—all innocence, frill and freckles—ask me not what became of him, 'cos I don't know. He was took away—far away, and I, *I* was left alone with my own dark thoughts, a small looking-glass, and my own 'orrid reflections. Rosa, my 'art is full and my 'ome is empty. Be my bride. All I have I lay at your feet. It ain't much, but it will serve to keep the wolf from the door; for, mark me, I shall not live

G

long; about sixty-five more years will finish *me* off.
You will then be able to choose a youthful bridegroom,
more suited to your age.

Rosa. (*aside*) The prospect is tempting—but oh, Lorrimor!

Growls. Remember how kind I have been to you, how
I have winked at your being late in the field, and how
when a remorseless master has compelled me to adminis-
ter chastisement to you I have dispersed the blows as
much as possible over your beautiful black—I mean back.
It always went against me to do it.

Rosa. I beg your pardon, it went against *me*.

Growls. Girl, your replies madden me. You must and
shall be mine.

Duet.

Lubly Rosa, Sambo scum,
Isn't fit to wed you——

Rosa. (*with intelligence above her station*) Tum, tum, tum.
Growls. Say, you'll wed your faithful Growls
He's got a tea-pot and six tow'ls.
Oh, Rose, cold black Rose,
I'm brimful of affection from my topknot to my toes.

Rosa. You plead with an eloquence few women could
find it in their hearts to resist, but——

Growls. Then away to a happier clime with me, where
the boathook grows on the ketchup tree; where the roaring
wind on the billowy deep keeps infant kids from their
beauty sleep; where the wild bee hums all the newest airs,
and the mustard plant grows thick on the stairs; where
the possum hops in his light canoe, and the bounding
brothers of Cariboo toss cabers high in the blithesome glee;
where the oozly bird and the lively flea, the whistling
oyster, the golden fleece, the great balloon, and the new
police, dance round and round to a Christmas tune, while
the street boys bellow out "Yar bar-loon," and the youthful sprigs of the house of Smith are sent with slaps up to
bed forthwith, and the maid of Athens entwines her locks
with pages torn out of Box and Cox, where all is revelry,
all delight—will you come, my Rosa, so right and light;

will you come, my Rosa, and off we goes—a—if you'll be
Growls's *cara sposa.*

ROSA. (*overcome by the rhyme*) Oh! (*faints*)

    (GROWLS *lifts her up and is about to carry her off when
    he is intercepted by* CINCINNATUS, L., *a young black*)

CIN. Hold, Growls!

GROWLS. Who are you calling old?

CIN. Am I not a man and brother?

GROWLS. No, you ain't.

ROSA. (*reviving*) Hah, that mysterious young negro
who has done nothing but haunt me——

GROWLS. P'r'aps he's haunt Sally; yet, no, she was a
woman, and *he*—he is——

CIN. A man and a brother.

ROSA. (*to* CINCINNATUS) Oh, save me.

CIN. I will die in your defence or perish in the attempt.

    (GROWLS *whistles—the stage is immediately filled by*
    OVERSEERS, SLAVES, *etc.*)

GROWLS. Seize that man. (*three* OVERSEERS *who attempt
it are immediately knocked-over-seers*—GROWLS *to* SLAVES)
There are four hundred of you; every one of you lay hold
of that fellow's collar.

PETE. (*a venerable* NEGRO) No, Mas'r Growls, can't do
it, Mas'r Growls, die rader than disobey Mas'r; Pete chop
of his right hand rather than disobey Mas'r; Pete go

through fire and water for Mas'r; but before Pete raise him hand 'gainst Cincinnatus, Pete see Mas'r——

CIN. Stay! fetch me a basin of warm water——

ALL. Hah!

CIN. And a piece of soap.

ALL. Hoh!

CIN. And a rough towel.

ALL. Hooh!

   (*intense excitement whilst the basin is brought*)

GROWLS. (*aside*) I begin to——

PETE. So do I.

ROSA. So do I.

EVERYBODY. So do we all!

   (CINCIN. *looks up with his face a pale brown*)

ROSA. Hah! can it be?   *Lor*——

   (CINCIN. *looks up with his face a paler brown still*)

ROSA. RI——   (CINCIN. *looks up clean*)

ROSA. MOR!!! *(faints)*

CIN. Yes, it is your own Lorrimor; anxious to see how you behaved yourself in the humble capacity of a cotton picker, I assumed the garments and hue of a man and brother, and amply have I been rewarded for my bold determination. Rosa, you are an ornament to any society. You shall be educated in French, Italian, German, the use of the globes and conic sections. In about twenty years you will be a fitting bride for me.

ROSA. (*delighted*) So soon!

GROWLS. (*aside*) Ha! ha! *I* shall not live to witness

their happiness; I will starve myself into a premature de-
cline.   (*retires to back and commences*)

LORRIMOR. And now, let one of the stirring ditties of
the melodious cotton pickers wind up the proceedings of
the day.

Finale.

Dance and sing
Ebery ting,
Makes de nigger cheerful,
And ob joy
Without alloy,
'Pon our honours we're full.
Bring de corn and make de mush,
Bring the drink and make de lush,
Heads as rough as scrubbing-brush,
Shins so black and tender;
Heel and toe it Sambos all,
Keep alive de nigger ball,
Rosa we a credit call,
To de female gender.
Dance and sing, &c.

Grand Negro Ballet, concluding with picture ; LORRI-
MOR *standing supper,* ROSA *standing on her toe, and*
GROWLS (*already much thinner*) *standing on his
dignity—Black Fire and*

Curtain.

www.ingramcontent.com/pod-product-compliance
Lightning Source LLC
Chambersburg PA
CBHW022344020726
47500CB00004B/1266